MW00638562

Secrets Of A Jewel

Sincerely,
Juliet C.

Secrets Of A Jewel

This book is a work of fiction. All names, characters, places and incidents are products of the author's imagination or are used fictitiously to protect the actual parties involved. Any resemblance to actual events or locales, or persons living or dead, is entirely coincidental.

All rights reserved, including the right to reproduce this book or portion thereof in any form whatsoever.

Copyright ©2017 by Juliet C. # 1-4382851941
PO Box 620624
Orlando, FL 32862
www.secretsofajewel.com

DEDICATION

Mami, I could write this entire book about the love and admiration I have for you and it still it wouldn't be enough. Your fortitude and resiliencies are traits that you have bestowed upon me, carving me into the person I am today. The examples you've exemplified have been my guide in life. You are the epitome of beauty and strength. Thank you for passing on your infectious smile, style and grace. Often times I'm asked about my confidence. It's because of you! The love, reassurance and encouragement you fostered within me as a child will always remain. Mami, tú eres la mejor!

My sister, you are blessing to me. You're my infinite friend, confidante and adviser. I appreciate your bold honesty. Thank for always having my best interests at heart, pushing me and believing, I can move mountains. Words will never translate sufficiently into the joy of having such an amazing sister in my corner. Our bond will last throughout eternity. I love you and my nephews dearly.

Papi, so much of me is you. You are loving, giving and full of charisma. I've always admired your business savvy, your ambitious and entrepreneurial mentality, all traits that I'm fortunate to have inherited. I love you.

My best friend, my love: It's been amazing epitomizing the significance of a healthy, fun and lasting relationships with you. Your support is invaluable; thank you for believing in me and creating a path for me to soar. You have inspired my vision more than you'll ever know. I love you!

To all my readers and supporters, thank you for joining me in my pursuit to inspire love and empower women. I drew the map to reach my destination. The path has not always been straight or smooth, but with every stop or stumbling block along the way, I have been determined to reach it without giving up or turning back. I appreciate you all coming along for the ride! I'm fortunate to have you travel this journey with me!

Brenda, the Booty Call

It's 2:54 a.m. Three text messages and a picture of his penis! What the hell am I supposed to do with that? I hopped out of bed and quickly jumped up. My house was still in shambles from the last time he was here. There were laundry and toys all over the floor. Some dirty plates and cups were still in the sink and my panties were tossed on the chandelier dangling, just how he had left it the last time he was here. Even though he never pays attention to what my house looks like, and he never bothered to care, I thought I might as well just tidy it up so he wouldn't think that I'm as nasty with cleaning as I am in bed during sex. Well, that's a different kind of nasty anyway. Tonight I was hoping he would sleep over. It would be nice to get up and make him breakfast for once. Some pancakes, eggs, steak...all the things real couples do the morning after. He promised me he would, so I was hoping that I could give him just enough of this sweet pussy to lock him in for the night! The only time he pretends to be in love with me or can look me in my eyes is when I'm riding his dick, but tonight, all that's about to change.

I spent about 45 minutes in the shower just prepping for this session with him. I had to make sure I was cleaned thoroughly and I couldn't afford to leave any stones unturned. Last time he wanted to do a little anal. I was not expecting that, so, this time I wanted to make sure I was on point. I crossed every T. I made sure every piece of hair on my body was shaved. I used the Q-tip in those not- too- easy- to- reach area, and soaked my lower body for a good 20 minutes, just in case he wanted to do something special. I wasn't taking any chances. Ass crack was squeaky clean and every corner was hair-free and sparkling. He would always lie to me that he had never "gone down" on any woman. Well, I was going to change his mind tonight! I made a light enough dinner so he'd be able to enjoy a taste of my cooking, but not get too full where we couldn't have fun and shake that ass in the sheets. The aromatic candles were lit and Netflix was ready. I had just put my purple silk sheets on the bed, my baby pink satin lingerie was hugging my hips and I was smelling like sweet, sugary chocolate. My makeup and hair were laid; all I needed was to be finally treated just like how I felt. Like a lady!

I wanted to make love tonight, real passionate love. wasn't even quite sure what that meant. I was wondering if it felt like the love-making scenes you see in the movies when they have the wine bottles on ice, feeding strawberries to one another, slow music, oil massages...Was that it? Or was it the same old thing that I was familiar with but just had another name. Like the hard, rough pussy pounding I was use to. Well, I was ready to find out.

By now I was so used to having sex after midnight, for anywhere between 20 to 30 shameful minutes, or could be less depending on how quickly he had an orgasm to be done with me. Just another routine. I'd get on my knees, suck him up, get poked and fondled and then we'd do it wherever there was a place to lie down. On the carpet, the cold concrete, the bathroom floor, anywhere. There was no cuddling afterward, no kissing during or after, and no showers before leaving. He'd put on his clothes, tap me on the shoulder to get my attention, force a dry detached smile, throw me up the deuces and then he's gone.

I hated how I felt when he was done with me. I always felt like a nobody, a nasty whore, a piece of meat! Thank God we only did it in the dark because I would spend a lot of time crying when he was on top of me or behind me. I knew better and deserved something more intimate and special, but I accepted it anyway because it made him feel good, and I was all about pleasing him. I made every man I ever slept with feel good. I had good sex and I was happy that I knew how to make a man feel good. I prided myself on having a bomb pussy. It offered me the confirmation I need to feel good about myself. But tonight should be different; it was time for a change, time for the cards to reshuffle. Here it goes....

About an hour passed by and I finally sent my reply "come thru." He was there in a flash; you would think that this man was waiting outside in my fucking complex. My incenses were lit, the candles were placed in the four corners and the table was set and ready. The atmosphere was right! I could see him looking a bit uncomfortable but I didn't sweat it. And before he could ask, "What's all this for?" I immediately explained that I wanted him and me to have a special night. He seemed annoyed and started giving me the run down that he wasn't hungry, didn't like the smell of my candles and how he had seen every Netflix movie I was suggesting. Again, it felt like all he wanted was sex tonight. I just wasn't feeling it and I was becoming a bit embarrassed. I looked way too pretty to just be sucking a dick, turn over like a dog only to get some gooey cum squirted into my mouth and onto my back. He peeped my attitude and must have felt sorry for me, so he agreed to cuddle me in the bed. Damn...finally, I was getting some foreplay! I started to feel really good as he began caressing and rubbing me all over. Perhaps he was going to take it slow or maybe, just maybe, he was going down below tonight. My thoughts were racing. It would be nice if I could have an orgasm for once. I needed to get mine, too! I was being carried away by my stupid thoughts and hopes, and before I knew it, he pulled my panties to the side and stuck his big, hard dick in. OUCH! I wasn't hardly even wet. Two seconds of foreplay and he banging the daylight out of me? No eye contact, no caressing, no kissing... just raw, hardcore, rough pounding, with groans and sweat dripping from his head to mine...3...2...1...ugh! He exploded all over my neatly shaved vagina. In no time he jumped up. Wow, he didn't even bother to grab a piece of paper towel to wipe me down. I wiped it off with my bed sheet and felt like some toilet seat with spilled urine on it. I felt so low, so worthless! He asked me if I minded him taking a shower. Well, it was the first time he was asking me that, but I figured he needed to get my perfume off of him before going home to his wife, who he claimed he was not really with, they were just "living under the same roof."

I was, as usual, hurt and humiliated. I attempted to hide my face as he was coming out of the shower because I didn't want him to see me in shambles. I wanted to appear indifferent. I wanted him to think that I wasn't in the least bothered by how he treated me, and that the feeling was mutual. But deep down I was hurting. But you know what, why cry over the situation? It wasn't going to change.

I thought for a minute and, then, I glanced across the room, and the grand idea hit me...the candles are still lit, the room is still fragrant, I can re-warm dinner and call someone else over. I'll just stroll through my contact list and see who was up and looking for a good time. So, he threw on his shirt, zipped up his pants, grabbed his keys and, again, gave me his signature deuces. "I'll check you out later," he said, and with that, he sped out the door. Deep down I knew he would be back. In a few weeks the texts would be pouring in again, harassing me about coming over for his quick fuck. Again I was trying to convince myself that I wouldn't fall for his bullshit, even though I've said it a million times. I sat on the couch looking puzzled, lonely and like a damn fool. And, before the tears could fall...knock...knock.... There was a loud bang on the door. He came back! My heart was screaming, "Wow, he came back!"

I quickly opened the door and there he was again. Maybe this time he thought about it and he wanted more… maybe he wanted to spend the night after all, I was thinking. "Hey, I…I…I think I left my phone; can you call it for me yo?" He appeared nervous and fidgety. I felt like a damn idiot. "Yo?" I knew he wasn't coming back to chill with me, not unless he was ready for a steamy, session two of sex again, and, like I said, that only happens every three or five days when he gets tired of his wife, I'm assuming. So, again, I pretended not to be bothered. "I'll call it for you," I said. "I hear it, I hear it, maybe it dropped behind my bed."

I reached in quickly to grab it before he could. My eyes glimpsed the screen, and the words across it caught my attention: "Brenda, the Booty Call." This dude had me saved as "Brenda, the fucking Booty Call!" Really?

Dear Brenda,

There's some much I can say but I'll start with what's most cliché: "Know Your Worth." You are so much better than 20 minutes of pleasure in the sheets. You desire to be loved, but a man can't give you what you can't give yourself and that's self love--which is the greatest love of them all. Don't compromise your values and betray your ideals.

Next time, let him know that you are not a midnight booty call. You have self pride and self-worth!

If a man wants you, he will make it his priority to be with you and to treat you like a woman and not a piece of ass. And, if he doesn't, then, there's no mistaking: He'll make it his priority to get rid of you. Because when you don't answer the late night texts or calls, please believe the next Brenda will. A man is only going to do what you allow him to do. What will you allow? Brenda, now is time to put the fire out.

Your character, self- worth, reputation and so much more

is burning...and the booty call attached to your name needs to go down in the flames.

Sincerely,

Juliet C.

Drunk Danielle

I could barely catch my balance as I stumbled inside the house. Frantically, I searched for the keys inside my purse and almost staggered over the rail in the process. I tried to vomit again, and there it was, slimy stomach contents splattered all over the parking lot and onto the asphalt. The neighbors were used to the stained concrete and I was accustomed to being the talk of the neighborhood anyway, so, nothing new. My face had been shamed many times before and it seemed that tonight would be no different.

For a second, I was seeing double and I couldn't distinguish between the door knob and the mailbox. Was this a shadow coming toward me? Wait...I was tripping. I finally stuck my keys in and opened the door. As soon as I walked inside our house, I smelled a bitch...I knew another woman had been here. Whether it was my female intuition or a sixth sense, something was fishy.

The smell of her perfume was still sitting in my living room. Or was I smelling my own fragrance again?

I couldn't think straight but I was looking for a reason to take my alcohol out on someone and Mikey was my target. Well, drunk or not, a bitch was inside my house! "Mikey... Miiikey!" I screamed. I was right behind him. I started in on his ass as soon as he walked out of the room. The nerve of him to be asking me what was my damn problem as if he thought I was stupid or something. "You were drinking again, weren't you?" he asked calmly. The calmer he appeared, the more my suspicion grew, and the more suspicious I became, the more my anger and frustration intensified. He was hiding something....and this time I knew it was more than my bottle of vodka.

I charged at him, speech slurred, spitting and foaming and hands outstretched ready to rip him to shreds. It was déjà vu. Another Friday would soon end with the police writing a report and Mikey having me arrested or escorting me out of our home.

I knew I needed to control my actions but the Patron was sinking into my ass and I just couldn't help myself. I started slapping him around, hitting, kicking, hissing and swearing as I threw a few man punches on his ass. Nothing landed. Instead, Mikey backed up and shoved me to the couch, asking me if I was OK in the process.

"Take it easy, hun, please," he whispered calmly. But I wasn't about to take anything easy. I grabbed a knife off the counter and clutched it tightly, aiming at him. All that time my head was spinning. I stood still trying to catch my balance as I began reaching in to stab him. Last year I missed his vein by an inch, this time, I swear, I was determined not to miss. I thought for sure he'd leave me then but he didn't. Well, I guess I scared his ass real good, so, sure enough, I was trying my luck another night.

"Ay, dios mío. No esta noche," he started speaking to me in Spanish. Yep, he was getting pissed because he was speaking his native tongue. Mikey reached for his phone. "Put your phone down!" I yelled. He began explaining and describing to the dispatcher about my behavior. I was angry that I couldn't understand a word he was telling her. "Por favor ayudáme. Está loca." Whatever he was saying was making me pissed as hell, but I knew he wasn't going to press charges. He would never!

Something inside of me wanted to stop but my fury kept egging me, so I continued; besides, I get away with anything with Mikey, so, there was no stopping me. He walked out the front door hoping I would keep my drunkenness inside the house. But I didn't. Instead, I followed right behind him with that sharp 10-inch knife in my hand. I didn't care if any of the nosy-ass neighbors heard me, I was going in for the kill. We stood there, right in the yard, fighting. I was the aggressor and he tried to do everything to back me off but I wouldn't. By this time a crowd began to gather and I was enjoying slapping Mikey around, watching him purr like a damn cat and seeing the feeling of anger and disgust from the crowd only spurred me on.

Then the whispers, "This drunk bitch is at it again... she's making a complete ass of herself...What is a man doing with a woman like this...What a party whore...damn, it shudda been me...I'd whoop her ass...bitch!" The comments wouldn't stop and I wasn't letting up either! The liquor riled me up and made me aggressive, delusional and irrational. But it was my therapy and it helped me cope and get through my pain. The more I screamed at Mikey, the more I pissed up myself. Then, I peed on myself again.

"Where is the whore you had in our home, Mikey? Where is she?" He would not reply. He turned around and made his usual head gesture. I could tell he was disgusted and embarrassed by my behavior. I wanted to be humiliated with myself but my pride and conscience were gone, so I couldn't find any other emotion but to cry.

His head nod continued and then, he mumbled, "I...I've had enough, I can't do this anymore." He had said that many times before but there was just something different about how he said it this time. His facial expression, his tone, his voice...his time he meant it and I could tell beyond a doubt that he was serious. I tried to curse at him but instead of curse words, more vomit came up.

Last time I stained the carpet; this time I stained his shirt. I threw up everywhere. It seemed he had had enough. Every time I tried to walk away, the Cîroc in me screamed at him, louder, taunting him, humiliating and cursing at him. It wasn't me. I wasn't myself. Blame it on the alcohol.

My head was spinning; I knew this feeling all too well. He didn't even bother to wait for the police. Neither did he even bother to help me back into the house. He just walked away, hurt, mocked...pain in his eyes.

For the first time I felt his hurt. There was turmoil raging within me. My heart was heavy. Then, amidst the confusion, my ears picked up the wailing of the sirens as they blasted the night sky. It was the police. Same story, same officer. Office McDonald stepped out of her car and began to address me. "Every weekend it's the same thing. I'm here writing a report because of you and this domestic disturbance. A man doesn't want a woman who goes out and parties and gets drunk every weekend. Look at you, woman, you smell like urine! Pissy drunk, one shoe on, froth at your damn mouth and blood-shot eyes. Your hair is completely disheveled and you look as though you haven't showered in a week! Aren't you tired of turning up. Don't you think it's time to turn down? A man doesn't want to be with someone who's always lit, has no self-control and can't stay away from damn alcohol, even an empty bottle. You're a damn disgrace!"

For the first time the Hennessy was quiet enough for me to listen and the liquor gave me a chance to hear her speak. She was right. What was I doing? Mikey was so frustrated that he wouldn't even give a report. I looked around at all the neighbors staring at me in disbelief. I was completely humiliated. Then, out of nowhere, I came under conviction. Whatever evil spirits had consumed me, whatever demons had robbed me of all common sense and human pride and dignity, had somehow relieved me. In that very moment, something else enveloped my existence, took control of my life. I began sobbing, I held out my hands to him, but he backed away. I realized what I was doing to him...to myself. I wasn't in a relationship with Mikey. I was in a relationship with alcohol. It was my drug. The only person who was cheating was me.

On Monday it was cognac; Tuesday I kissed tequila; Wednesday I made out with whisky; Thursday I slept with rum; Friday I cuddled with Cîroc; and Saturday and Sunday I had a euphoric combination of them all. I needed help.

"Well, I can't take you to jail like I had planned because Mickey is refusing to give a statement, but I am going to advise you to get your life together because the next time I'm called out here, it won't be nice," the officer warned. She further insisted on dropping me off at a hotel that night to give Mickey some space and time to cool off. I was praying he would. Before I got out of her police car, she handed me a card with some poignant words.

"Listen," she said calmly and reassuringly. "I had a problem. The same problem you had and it helped me. Now, I don't have this problem anymore. I've been alcohol free for six years. Try this. I'm sure you're tired of this lifestyle. I'm an officer, but I'm a person, a woman, and I want to help you."

Admittedly, Officer McDonald was sure right. I checked into my room, slept the liquor off, jumped up the next morning and caught a cab to the address on the card. I walked timidly into the building. It was just simple and plain on the outside. Gray paint stripping off at the sides and some neatly trimmed shrubs decorated the half paved path that led up to the door. I paused, looked around and continued. Inside there were people who looked just like me. Broken, scared, wretched and helpless. They were all there and I felt ashamed but relieved. I needed help. I joined them around the circle and introduced myself to the group.

"Hi," I said timidly, clenching my palms, embarrassed. "My name is Danielle...err...Drunk Danielle and I'm here because I have a drinking problem."

In chorus they all shouted, "Welcome to Alcoholic Anonymous, Danielle. Drunk Danielle."

Dear Danielle,

There's nothing like a sleek glass of wine to get you in the mood. And, there's equally nothing like a couple shots of Patron to get you turned up, making you the life of the party. However, there's a time and place for them both, so know your limits and set your boundaries. A man enjoys a woman who likes to have a good time and isn't afraid to kick off her heels and dance. He likes a real woman, nothing pretentious. However, that doesn't mean that you have to stand on the bar and do it. Know what your body can handle, work within your limits and stick with that.

Partying with your girlfriend is cool but it shouldn't happen every night or weekend. Set aside some time for your man. They love to see our different "shades" or sides. Just don't be too hyperactive and hyperbolic, exaggerating who we are; it's not necessary.

We want to take them on a ride but we don't want to drive them away. Be real. Be you!

Sincerely,

Juliet C.

Settling Selena

All I ever wanted to do was to get married, but the thought of this was more like a marathon, a test of endurance for which I was psyching myself both physically and emotionally. Only it was proving to be more of an emotional torture. I would always fantasize about the proverbial "Mr. Perfect, my Knight in Shining Armor." And, now, I'm starting to realize that these fairytale endings are only written in children's books. No Prince Charming is ever going to bring me my glass slipper, and no bell would ring at 12 and turn me into a princess. I've been in love at least 17 times, and it seems as though at least two of them were almost "committed relationships." Or so I thought. Truth is, I'm not infatuated with the idea of marriage but, neither am I good at being single. But when all was said and done, I want a ring on it. That single life just isn't for me.

Every time I look around or log onto some social media account, another one of my friends is getting married, in love, in some relationship or...just happy. And here I am, stuck, looking single and displaced. I knew deep in my heart that I had done everything to get a man and to keep one, but it felt like every time I think I'm getting serious with someone...Boom! Just like that, it's over. I just wanted a piece of a man. You see, a "piece of a man" was better than no man at all. Unfortunately, I was buying into that idea, too. Someone I can cuddle with, especially at night, cook for, go on dates with, make a few love posts about (even if I'm lying). Just someone to call my own.

I'd reached a point in my life where I really didn't care anymore. For one, I had to stop being picky and settle for someone who shared my dreams and was ready for some commitment. I had promised myself that the next man I met I would compromise on my "standards." I was willing to negotiate if I really wanted something to materialize. I eventually realized that that was part and parcel of the problem why I just couldn't connect with the right man. I was too consumed into certain misconceptions that he must be tall, educated, have his own place, two kids maximum, no baby mama drama, must have a car... and the laundry list continued! Well, enough of that. It was me. Nothing is wrong with being selective in a man choice, but I guess I had taken things way too far. I'm just tired of dragging my lonely ass home every night and the only thing I had to hug was my pillow.

I had spent the last seven months single. And, yes, everything about being single depressed me. I work hard, I have two college degrees and I'm a damn good mom. My boys just need a good dad because their daddy is trifling, and it seemed like every time I introduced them to someone new, it never worked out.

So I met Bobby about a year ago at a gas station. I was wearing the cutest little red shorts and matching bikini top as I headed inside to put 40 dollars on number seven. I saw him staring at me the moment I pulled up. I knew he was checking out this body. What in the world was he doing at the gas station, I thought. Well, I didn't know and I sure didn't care. The only thing I noticed was his shiny black Range Rover, his broad shoulders and thick, sexy lips. Out of all my very many relationships, no man had ever offered to pay and pump my gas, so I started to feel really special. My two boys sat in the car and Bobby even ran a few jokes with them. Now, if I could find a father figure for my two nuggets that would be even better. My babies' daddy is still two years behind in child support, still two months late in picking the boys up for the park and it's the end of the school year and I'm still waiting for his sorry ass to bring the school uniforms over! Bobby was somehow different. More like the whole package. And I wanted to have that package so badly!

We exchanged numbers immediately and that marked the beginning of our love story. We spent every night on the phone. We talked about everything, from his failed NFL career to the arson attack on his Atlanta property. He left no stone unturned. I even googled him and saw where he almost made it. That was until he got into something petty with the law and, as you know, nowadays nobody wants to see a good man do good so, he had a criminal record that forced him to be hustling in between jobs and homes.

At one point he was living with his grandmother, cousin and even childhood friend. He sounded like a loser, I know, but like my pastor always says, "You gotta see a man for his potential," and that's what I saw in my Bobby. He had a lot of potential and I was glad I saw it in him. So, after three good weeks I felt like I could trust him. It goes without saying that I wasted no time in moving him in with me. The first three months felt like one big happy family. I reminded myself not to nag about standards, commitments and all that other stuff that seem to drive them away. Look, I had a man, and if I wanted to keep him, I had to be careful. I felt like a wife and that was a big deal for me!

Finally, I had someone I could come home to at night, especially after a hard day's work. Every woman needs that. It's a necessity! And it felt good! He'd drop the boys off to school in the morning, drop me off to work and then assured me he'd spend the rest of his time searching for a job. I'm never good in long-term relationships, so I needed to make sure that I didn't run this one away like I did all the others. So, I tried not to hasten to rush to conclusions. I tried to help Bobby find a job but there was no luck at all. Truth is, I wanted this so badly, especially for the boys that I didn't mind paying the bills. He was helping with the boys. He was good at cooking, helping with homework, running errands and house chores. He was holding things down from his end and I was pleased. So, don't label me as being desperate. He was short in the pocket but he was doing things no other man had ever done. When he wasn't doing chores or working with the kids, he would be outside playing cards or on the kids' video game.

I made sure, too, that I did everything a wife was supposed to do. No, I wasn't a "wife" yet, but I needed to prove to him so that I would qualify in case he wanted to pop the question. He was the perfect fit and he told me he was ready to settle down and eventually get married, too. "One day," he would say... And I believed him.

A year went by and he was still in between jobs. I was now

working my second job, paying all the bills and making sure I had my man's back. I would pay for our dates, family trips and even take him on shopping sprees whenever I got a bonus from work. Now, I know this may sound crazy because I'm the first to admit that domestic violence should not be condoned in any relationship, but when a man loves a woman and wants to support him so much it's hard, and, you know what? They get frustrated, which turns into anger and, eventually, abuse.

Admittedly, Bobby hit me quite a few times. I kicked him out on a number of occasions because I didn't want the boys to be in that kind of environment. I want them to grow up to be respectable men. Then, a day or two would pass and I want him back. After a few pleadings, a handpicked rose and an apology, he'd be right back home. I couldn't complain because at least I had a man...or, a piece of a man. And, I can't help but adding, the sex was great. Perhaps that was my weakness. I never thought that I would be that girl that I said I would never be. The one who works all day while her man doesn't, the girl who takes a few jabs, black eyes and busted lips, the woman who makes excuses for her man to justify why he has to beat the block, beat me or the woman who has settled all because she so badly wanted a man. But I had had enough.

I woke up one day and I was drowning in my tears. The concealer could no longer hide my bruises, and I could no longer hide my pain. I looked in the mirror and I didn't like what I was seeing. It was now two and a half years and I had no ring, I was flooded in bills, pregnant and at the risk of being kicked out by my landlord. They were sick of all the violence, the screams, slaps and bangings on walls and floors, the countless police calls and the recurring 10-day-or more late monthly rent.

I had lost my identity. This was a perfect case of desperate Settling Susie! That was me and who I'd become. I had bargained way beyond any sensible negotiation and was too willing to accept any and everything from a man. Had I compromised too much? Obviously, I had. Where were my morals, my self-respect and everything I stood for and believed in? I knew I was better than that, but I found it difficult to let go.

As time slipped by, the situation worsened, so, it was time for Bobby to go. There were no tears, no amount of apologizes and no hours of good sex that would change my mind. There's no denying that I didn't want to be in a relationship, I just wanted a healthy one. Again, I started to realize that there was nothing wrong with me having standards. There was absolutely nothing wrong in wanting a man who was a hard worker, a protector and provider. Someone who loved me unconditionally and respected me enough to marry me and treat me how I am to be treated, who loved my kids like I love them, and who thought I was worthy enough to have his last name.

I knew immediately that the first step started with me. Before I could start a new relationship I had to first love myself and know my worth. So, you know what? I did something Bobby never thought I would do. Not even I thought I would. I packed up all our possessions, took my two boys and left. Not only was I leaving the man that never loved me, hurt me, lied to me and abused me but, more importantly, I was leaving ME, I was leaving behind the pathetic and insecure and desperate woman I had become. The woman that threw away everything just to be in a "relationship," just for a happy ending that never ends happily when they start the way ours did. Essentially, that was what I was leaving. I had finally mustered the courage to bring an end to a tumultuous relationship.

If I wanted to see a new woman in the mirror, one who knew her worth, I needed to change, and that's what I did. Then it happened. I woke up to a new me. I didn't realize how many years I had spent dead. Seems I was emotionally, spiritually and intellectually comatose during all these years. I had a difficult time even attempting to figure out what had really happened to me. It was much bigger than my failed relationship with Bobby. This was years and years of looking for a man to validate and reassure me and, more importantly, to love me. Maybe it was because I didn't have a father that I felt that love from, so I spent years searching for it. Or maybe I didn't feel worthy or deserving enough of being happy, so I was too willing to settle for society's rejects, the substandard, the ones who nobody else desired. Even though I was always reassured of my physical beauty, I never felt very pretty, very smart, very nothing. But I now know that a man can't help me love me. I have to love me, to feel that I'm beautiful and smart and everything that's desirable. If I don't first feel that way, and If I don't see that jewel when I look in the mirror, no man is going to see it either.

My next relationship is with myself. And I won't settle for anything less. It goes without saying that if I hold myself to a high standard, then I most certainly will hold my man to it, too. If I work, he's going to work; if I pay bills, we pay bills; if I want more for myself, he will have to want more for himself too; if I'm building an empire, we are both building an empire; and if I love me, then he has to love me, too. Nothing is singular around here anymore. There's nothing more attractive, more sexy, more fulfilling than knowing your worth. If I know it, then he will definitely know it, too.

Now, it's time to be me again. I have no choice but to go back to the drawing board and, once again, raise the bar. My standards are high and they won't be compromised. If a man isn't comfortable with these "requirements" or willing to aspire to meet them, then, clearly, he's not the one for me.

Life teaches us many lessons, and one very important one I've learned is when the race seems long, never give up. If your energy is drained and life seems unbearable, keep going. If the odds are against you, just keep running 'til you reach the finishing line.

Dear Selena,

Many times love makes you settle. And oftentimes we settle for less than we bargained for. Invariably, we do it because we see what the person can be and not necessarily what they are, what they can have and what they may not be able to achieve or not achieve. All of this is fine. Being optimistic about someone you love and potentially seeing yourself with is the right way to go about things.

However, also remember that you don't have to compromise your standards to accommodate anyone. The person you love has to be willing to stand, be assertive and embrace you and your struggles and, if they can't, then they'll have to jump, walk or crawl to get there. If they love you, they will. As long as you set attainable and realistic goals, it will materialize. It's not about lowering your ideals, but it's also certainly not about settling for less. Know what you want, be aggressive and stick to your convictions. Declare your expectations and priorities at the beginning of the relationship so that it's clear on both sides. There must be transparency on either end; know what you want. Don't make up things along the way and change up the "menu" unexpectedly just because things may or may not be going your way and expect him to just fall in line. Remember, he's not a puppet. Communicate.

Sincerely,

Juliet C.

Paranoid Paula

I waited all night to hear back from Justin's lying ass. Where the fuck was he? Studio sessions are timely, but you do get breaks. He could've at least called me. A few more minutes and I was about to hop in my ride, drive to the studio, drag a bitch from off her knees, and shut that recording session down. He knows I'm good for it!

I was trying to give him the benefit of the doubt, but fuck that! His ass should've been home by now. I know he was working but I expected him to be home by a certain time. What in the hell could be taking him so long? Ugh! A myriad of thoughts raced through my mind. The session ends at 9:30 and it was now 9:32 p.m. And, yes, I'm aware that it's only two minutes, but knowing his sneaky ass, he can do a lot of damage during that time, and worse, considering his past history, he's expected to account for every fucking second. I had to know where he was at all times, I didn't care a fuck, and it helped to put my mind at ease. Whatever insecurities I had were dispelled as long I kept a tab on his ass. He doesn't like to hear me bitch and moan, and this explains why he normally calls or texts me to let me know his whereabouts. Frankly, keeping tabs on him is not something he appreciates, but I see the need to make sure he isn't up to something because he can be very sneaky. Whenever I question him about what he's doing or whom he's with, I can almost see the tension and anger festering inside him, indirectly warning me to back off and stop treating him like a damn child. He values when I'm not policing him and is able to trust him in spite of his past. But like many other nights, tonight was a night I simply could not help myself and I began to feel a bit inquisitive as to where he was.

I was 10 seconds away from speed dialing his manager when he walked through the door all soaked and looking like a wet dog. He had better been running from a pit bull or the Devil himself to explain why he was soaking wet. My roving eyes examined every detail on his body, furiously searching for anything out of place. My nose was on the job, carefully sniffing him out like I was a special agent for the K-9 unit as I waited for an excuse. All kinds of thoughts raced through my mind before I even greeted him. And when you think of it, a lot could've happened in two minutes and, knowing him, I wasn't taking any chances. Hell, he probably stopped to get his dick sucked on the way home, who knows? I demanded to know where he was all that time. I didn't care if it was a massive 10-car pile-up on the fucking highway and it and was shut down, he should have at least called to let me know!

He lied so much you could never really tell with him. Even when he might probably been telling the truth you still couldn't know because lies were a part of his DNA. I wanted so badly to erase his past, but in my mind he was still lying, cheating or just being sneaky, so when it came to him, you had to assume the worst. And I did.

And so his story began. He stammered and paused in between his drama as he recounted his last two minutes. As soon as he started with his excuse, I cut him off immediately. His version usually sounded too much like it was coming straight out of a fairytale and I wasn't in for any lame excuses again. Well, not tonight. No matter what he said, somehow I had this deep intuition that on his way home he had made a quick stop by some bitch's house. That's how men usually do it--at least from my experience. He knew I didn't believe him and so he was laughing at me, making me look stupid. He always said I accuse him of every damn thing, and it takes nothing for my mind to go into overdrive. But truth is, my mind wanders off on its own, thinking all kinds of shit when he's not home and worse when he's late. Deep down inside I was relieved that it was only a few minutes and not an entire night.

However, I was still suspicious that he was lying about something, and knowing him, I was probably right. I couldn't wait for him to remove his clothes so I could sniff them out. This nose doesn't lie. I know how the studio smells. So, it wouldn't be hard telling the difference between a true studio session, studio sex, studio ass, studio pussy or studio groupies, and if I suspected anything besides a music session, I was going to fuck him up.

Justin had cheated on me too many times to the point where I had lost count. So, I wasn't going to be naive and allow this to happen to me again. I had endured enough embarrassment, walking around like a jackass while my man was cheating on me. By now I knew all the signs; I sniffed them all out. And, tonight, I was sniffing again!

Admittedly, I was very insecure. And being a former model, it didn't really help me in this regard. Conversely, it kind of minimized how I really defined myself. I'm not perfect, but having this kind of status makes you prone to public scrutiny at all times. It further projects you into the limelight and onto a public platform where the world is watching you and expects you to look perfect. This industry is filled with lots of competition and I felt like I wasn't striking a balance. Instead, I was in a losing race where I had to make sure that my man kept his eyes on me and his dick in me...and only me! I had no time for further exploits in trying to determine if he was creeping. Not again. I know I look good, that wasn't under contemplation. I've always been sexy, but after getting older and dealing with a man that I couldn't really trust, I started to feel like less of myself and more like a paranoid, miserable woman. That was me! Eventually, all of the stress weighs you down physically, mentally and emotionally. Well, it was weighing pretty heavily on me and I blamed Justin. He was the source of my insecurities and my paranoia. Had he been faithful like I was, he wouldn't have to worry about me treating him like a boy instead of a man. Maybe if he had learned his lesson the first time to save his love and loyalty for me only, this wouldn't have happened. Instead, he chose to share it with other women. So, you can understand why he is always under scrutiny and I have to be checking him and smelling his draws every time he took them off! Yep, I made sure that I did my random boxer checks on his slick ass. At least his draws were clean and I didn't have to find skid marks and shit stains. Instead, I smelled for pussy juice just to make sure he wasn't fucking away like I suspected. Time and again I would meet upon a few unsightly stains, but I wasn't too concerned about that. A man has to shit, right? What I was more concerned about were the sights and smells caught up in his boxers that were obviously not mine but some other chick's. Or were they mine and I was just being paranoid again?

Everything had to be inspected when he came to him. A bitch might as well call me "Inspector Dick Gadget" because he wasn't getting away with shit again. Call me stupid if you want, but I even timed his cum. If he was a minute late in busting that nut, his ass was cheating! If his cum wasn't the right shade, amount or consistency, he was fucking somebody else! And, if you think that that was all, then you have a next guess coming. Check this...

If my phone tracker put him one mile out of range, he was cheating. If a follower on his social media clicked "like" or started following him, he was cheating. If he looked at another woman in public, he was cheating. If he wanted to hang out with his boys, guess what? He was cheating! Bitches in the studio...CHEATING! I didn't give a damn if they were recording a Grammy hit, if they were there while he was there, he was cheating! Even if he got too friendly with the waitress serving our food, he was cheating. I checked the trash, called and texted a million times, and if he didn't answer, I showed up to where he was and followed him around until all was clear. When he was asleep, I would sneak into the room until I got a hold of that phone. A lock code? I broke into that, too. There was no getting away with it anymore. I had missed many nights of sleep, making sure I knew his every move, and if a number looked unfamiliar or suspicious, I called it back immediately. Trust me, I had to make sure that Justin knew I wasn't going to accept him abusing and mistreating me anymore. And, so, this time I was a woman on a mission. I had had enough and there was no stopping me! I really didn't care if it wasn't practical or healthy, all I cared about was taking care of business, and making sure that my man was only my man and not another woman's. So, criticize me all you want and call me crazy in the head but it gave me satisfaction.

My plan was for us to be together, forever, and if we were going to be together, I needed to know his every move. He doesn't have to know mine; I wasn't the problem. He was the problem! My friends criticized me and called it a little ridiculous and over-the-top, and encouraged me to leave him if I didn't trust him. They chastised me for being my own private investigator, but by now I knew exactly how to figure out if he was up to something. They could continue judging me all they want. While they were miserable and crying over their cheating men, I was handling my own business. It was extra work, but, like I said, I was happy.

I used to be suspicious that he had slept with a woman in our house, in my bed. He swore to me that that was never the case and I believed him. But the cheating didn't stop. It only worsened. He promised me that he would never cheat again, and a big, desperate jackass like me always believed him. And every time I thought he was done with messing around, I was so wrong.

That skinny girl at the restaurant, a lady from the mall, the store assistant, the teacher from the baby's day care, my cousin, my friend, my niece's friend ...the list went on and on. This nasty bitch just wouldn't stop. I questioned everyone that bore an air of suspicion. So, it's not that I was crazy; it's just that I knew what I had on my hands. Why not just leave him? A rational thought, I guess. But here it is: I loved him and I couldn't leave him. No way! Judge me all you want. I wanted to be with him and him only and, I wanted us to be happy. I just couldn't bear him cheating on me again or accept the idea of him having another woman besides me, but what was I to do? I had gotten so sick of letting bygones be bygones. I felt stupid and simple for allowing him to play me like that, but I couldn't admit that to anyone. It was no secret that the whole world knew that I was a fool for letting this man try me over and over again. So, having him make a fool out of me again just wasn't an option. It's not like I enjoyed it but, truth is, I didn't want to lose him or to be laughed at. I was willing to act tough and pretend like all was well. He'd already taken me through enough; there wasn't much more that I could bear. Women playing on my phone, him posting up in the club with other women--you name it, he's done it!

Maybe he treats me like this because I don't have a ring on my finger. Well, it didn't matter. I'm his woman. Not some simple side chick that deserved to be abused. So, the time came for me to see if he was still up to his slimy ways. So, I decided to test his dumb ass to see if he had really changed.

I spent all Thursday creating fake pages on Instagram, Snapchat, Facebook and Twitter. I set the bait and was waiting for him to catch it. I used a fake picture I found online. Nice, round, plump ass, curly hair, hourglass body, mouth-watering Latina. He was into sexy women looking like me, so I knew if he was still up to his no- good ways then, it would be easy: He would swallow the bait, hook, line and sinker!

Paula was my profile name. He accepted all my requests on each site I requested him. It was working! I couldn't believe Justin had not changed one bit! I was glad the trick was working but at the same time I was very angry with this man. A man who I'd been grooming all this time, pampering and loving, still had intentions of sleeping with every ho in sight. After everything was perfect, I was ready to go. I dove straight into his Instagram DM with an evil, conniving grin on my face. I waited. After about 10 seconds this dude wrote back, "Hi, baby, hmmm...you looking good! Dammn!" That quick! Was he serious? This asshole just failed to realize that he wasn't going to get away with this again. What the fuck was taking me so long to realize that this man didn't care. Maybe I had annoyed him to the point where he didn't give a rat's ass anymore. I wasn't quite sure, however, how to feel at this point. Should I be mad, embarrassed, sad, indifferent? One thing for sure, my fingers were shaking, I was breathing hard because I was freaking pissed! If Justin was bold enough to DM someone whom he didn't know, then, just imagine how often he probably did that on a regular basis. I had gotten him! That bitch! And now I was catching him right in the act. I was about to reveal myself but that little demon on my right shoulder kept egging me on, and that's exactly what I did. He was at my throat, and I was complying. Asking me shit like, if I have a man, how old I was, where I lived, send him a picture of my pussy and my legs opened and when we can meet up. My blood was boiling. I had had enough. My poor heart was weak and shattered. And just like I knew it, it turned out well, I wasn't crazy after all. Truth is, I was dealing with a pathological liar, a sick man who couldn't help himself. At that point I wished if I could just jump through my phone screen like a genie and pluck out his fucking eyes! I wanted to scream, "I got you, bitch, I got you!" But I played cool, continued to catfish him in and lead him all the way on. I asked him if he had a girlfriend. He responded, "Yes, I have a girlfriend, someone whom I hurt, cheated on, did her wrong. Someone whom I love very much but she doesn't trust me at all. Someone who reminds me a great deal of you, Paula."

My heart skipped and I smiled. Damn...he knew it was me.

"Paranoid Paula, are you there? Baby, I love you. Please, baby, please forgive me, I'm trying. Don't think I'm caught. I knew it was you," he wrote back. And at that very moment, I knew it was time for my paranoid ass to either trust him or let him go.

Dear Paula,

There's an old quote that says, "A single lie discovered is enough to create doubt in every truth expressed." It's simple because I lied to you before, you think I'm always lying, right? There may be some logic behind that, but how fair is that? If you don't trust someone to the point where you are paranoid, jealous and miserable in your relationship, you must either let it go or work on the trust issues.

It's true...everyone doesn't change just because they say they changed and, yes, people need to be redirected to change. Change is a journey that begins with an individual. It is more than just saying, "I've changed." Essentially, I want you to show me and not just tell me. But we as women also have to be willing to let go off the past wrongs that he did and give him the chance to be real and a little of who you want him to be. Don't police your man. Move away from the 24-hour surveillance, checking his phone, stalking him, breaking into passwords, watching his every move or think that every woman he looks at, he wants. Maybe he does or maybe he wants only you.

But truth is, nothing is wrong with a man looking at another woman. Remember, this was how he spotted you in the first place, by admiring you! You have to know your man and if you can't trust him or you're not willing to trust him, be with someone whom you trust. But if your relationship is worth fighting for, then, fight and trust. Remember it takes a strong person to admit when they messed up but an even stronger one to accept a person after they have messed up. Decide what kind of person you want to be.

Sincerely,

Juliet C.

Money-Hungry Monique

The moment I fell from the womb, I was smelling dollar signs. Money. That was my motivation. When other little girls were playing with dolls, I was cutting out fake bills from magazines and newspapers and putting them in my little purse. My mom always said that money is the root of all evil, but for me, it was the root of happiness, prosperity and power. From the time I hit elementary school I rocked every pair of Jordan's. I was the first to be parading in them long before they even hit the stores. I sported the latest jewelry, had any toy I wanted, expensive cell phone, four gold teeth to the bottom of my grill--you name it, I had it.

My dad would drop me off every morning in his luxury ride and everyone would stop and stare, making me feel like the President's daughter. We had everything. Throughout the entire neighborhood we were known as the Joneses because we had it all and everybody wanted to keep up with us. My daddy had 12 baby mamas and 16 children and each of us was born with a silver spoon shoved into our mouths. My brothers and I never needed anything, and anything we wanted we got it. Being his youngest child and only daughter, his world revolved around me. I was his princess and he was my hero. We were inseparable. Talk bad about my dad and you'd see what happened. He could do nothing wrong; to me, he was perfect. There was never anything anyone could tell me about my daddy that was wrong. Never! Moses Jones was his name but the community affectionately called him "Mo Money Mo." So, now you'll understand why my mom named me Monique, and I was happy to be named after a man like my dad. My mom always warned me, "Make sure you stay away from a hustler like your no good, worthless Daddy." Back then, I wasn't quite sure what a hustler was, but the older I grew, the more I figured it all out. I couldn't understand why my mom had the nerve to call my dad worthless, good-for-nothing after all he did for us. He gave her a lot of money, expensive clothes, shoes, handbags and the new foreign cars he bought her every year. She was the only woman with a two-story, four-car garage who had a house with a pool in the hood. Strange that she never ever complained that he was a hustler, when he was bringing in all the money and giving her a life of luxury. She took all his cash and never murmured a simple "thank you." Daddy told me straight up that she was a hater and warned me not to be as miserable and ungrateful as she was.

I never repeated any clothes in school. I was always in the latest styles and followed the current trend. Everyone always seemed jealous of me and they all wanted my life. All the girls wanted to be me and all the boys wanted to be with me. I tried to stay clear of guys, but when I was in 8th grade I could no longer ignore the attention from the boys. There was only one guy that caught my attention and his name was David. I knew my dad didn't want me talking or dating anyone...EVER...but this guy was just everything. While he didn't quite fit the thug stereotype, he was weighing half-way between and I loved it. David had a nice, low haircut, with dollar signs designed in the back of his head, fresh pair of kicks, Cuban-link chain, and he smelled like the leather on my dad's convertible. I'm not sure what attracted me to him but it was something that made me feel really special. He was always calling me pretty, cute and buying me little gifts.

I guess I saw in him what I saw in my dad--money! I was always told by my dad to "marry the money and not the dude," but I was in love with David, so, for him, I was willing to make an exception. I thought David and I would be together forever and would one day get married. I had lost my virginity to him by the time I was 14 and I was hoping my daddy never found out. While my dad was taking care of his "business," David and I would be "experimenting" in bed. Daddy told me he was the CEO of his company now, and the less time at home, meant the more money in my pockets. Well, needless to say, I was cool with that because that meant more alone time with David.

After a while, my dad became aware that there was something up with David and me, and I think he started to accept it. Many people couldn't believe how accepting he'd become of him; even I was in shock. My mom was surprised when I told her that my dad would give David rides home from school and that David and my dad had become close. She'd always say to me, "Your dad must want something with that young boy. Moe, be careful, please be careful." Well, what the hell did I need to be careful for? After all, he was my damn daddy, and the more she made those stupid ass comments, the more I realized that Daddy was right about Mommy. She was miserable and a hater and I decided I wanted to move in with him full time. And so, after months of fighting with the courts, I finally did. Everyone was skeptical about my daddy gaining custody. They gossiped that he must have paid off the judge because he was an unfit father who should not have had such a privilege. But truth was, he was a great provider and, to me, there was nothing more fit than that. My mom would always tell me to "look past the money, Mo, and then you'll be able to see," but why would I look past money-- who does that? Only a broke bitch --and I was far from broke!

So, I was known as the famous "Lil Mo Money" all the way to my adult years. The years slipped by and I was 21 years old and driving a Porsche. I had been driving expensive whips since I was 16 and I never expected anything less. With Daddy's help, David and I moved into our beach front condo that was situated in the city near the suburbs. David and I were still rocking and, besides my dad, he was the next big man in town making money. What I liked most about him was the money he would give me, spend on me and spend for me. Whatever I asked for he made sure I had it . After a while he made a name for himself; everyone called him "David Dollaz." He was working for my daddy eight years now, and everything seemed smooth. I had it all: my man with money and my daddy. No complaints.

After all these years the secret was still buried, hidden deep within my daddy and David. No one knew how they made all this money. All I knew was that I just had to ask and my daddy would quickly pull out his wallet and inside it was a thick wad of cash, and now David was closely following behind him. Of course,

David's stack was never as big as Daddy's, but he was almost there. I was amazed that he carried so much money in his pockets and not in the bank. But he always told me to never question anything, and so I didn't push it. I had heard rumors about how they got their money, but I never believed it. Well, truth is, I didn't want to believe it. I was more interested in maintaining my lifestyle and I could only accomplish that with money. All my life that was all I knew and, at that point, I wasn't interested in knowing how it felt not to have money.

Dad used to tell me that his "career" was not up for discussion, and even though he couldn't teach me about his "job," he took me to his "school," the school of life. There he taught me all I needed to know in order to survive, he taught me about the joys of having money. He would say to me, "Mo baby, first, you get the money, then you get the world." And in my head, that was always my motto. He made me feel like the world was mine, and the only way to own it was to have money, and plenty of it.

And so the truth was ready to be told. One night David and I were returning from the movies. He slowed down, pulled the Benz over and said he wanted to talk to me. I could sense that the conversation was about to get a little uncomfortable because he seemed extremely nervous the entire time we were at the movies. He kept checking his phone, looking over his shoulder, and gazing at his watch. So, when he said he needed to talk, I became a bit uneasy. My mind was wandering and so I asked, "What's going on with you, Dollaz?" Then, he stared me in the eyes and mumbled firmly, his teeth gritting, "Mo, I want out. I got a lot of heat on me and I want out!" I stared at him, lost and confused. "Out of what, David?" I enquired. I had no clue what in the hell he was talking about. Then, he stared at me as if I were crazy and snarled, "Where do you think it's all coming from, Mo? I don't have a real job, your father has never had a real job. You can't be this blinded by money! I've been doing illegal jobs for your dad since I was 14. Your father, your hero, is the biggest scam artist in the hood and I want out but he won't let me and he's trying to make me do an exchange that could get me killed."

My mouth dropped. My daddy, a scammer? All these years and this was what he was doing? Scamming people, robbing, stealing, killing?

David told me a lot of things I could never have imagined about my dad, some real horror stories, I must say. I was very upset at what I was hearing and I could hardly respond. It wasn't just the reality of losing all my luxury that was torturing me, but it's the lifestyle that my dad was living. How could he?

It was a slow drive home and throughout the entire journey, my mind drifted on to the money and not David's fear. I couldn't help it. What was going to happen if my dad got caught, if we lost it all, if David got out? He said that either he stopped doing it or he was going to die. David was into some deep water. But, let's face it, was I willing to help him get out and slow down the money flow? Was his life more important than money? My dad was setting him up, probably to take over, and the more I thought about it, the more I realized that I didn't care where the money was coming from or how they were getting it, as long as he was still getting it, what difference did it make now anyway? He may as well stay in it and let the dollars flow. Damn! Once we pulled up to my yard, I was ready to respond to David.

My answer left him in total shock. "Listen, Dollaz, this is my life. I'm hungry for the money and I'm not willing to let it go. Whatever job my dad is asking you to do, just get it done. I'm not passing up any money and neither are you. It's time to put on your big boy pants; it's too late to stop now anyway. My dad has been good to you. So, just go with the flow, man, if not for him, just do it for me."

With that, David began twitching his eyes and wringing his hands. He couldn't believe it but, oh, well. I didn't believe it either. I wasn't about to let him ruin my status. My dad was obviously doing this since I was a child and, if it was OK for him as a grown ass man, then it should be OK for David. My dad had it all, it was David's time to stack up and he was passing him the torch. I got out of the car and left him in disbelief. I really didn't care what he thought; he is a man and he needed to think money and nothing else. Maybe I knew deep down that something was going on all along and just refused to accept it, maybe David was right. I WAS blinded by the money and all its trappings. Little by little it all started to make sense. The late night appointments and obligations my dad had, the exchange of bags and thick envelopes, the secret text messages, phone calls and the shoe boxes full of money. Money in the freezer, money in the walls, money in the attic and under the false flooring, various weird and hidden places throughout the house. The guns, the body guards...How did I miss it? Or did I deliberately and consciously turn a blind eye?

And now that I knew all the details of the job my dad wanted him to do, I needed to convince him to get it done.

That night I confided in my dad about David's concern. I also made him aware that I knew everything and that I wasn't upset. Thing is, I didn't want my daddy to be angry with David for spilling the beans, so I tried to be very diplomatic and leaned toward my dad's side and also carefully arguing David's position. I applauded my dad instead for putting money before his life and thanked him for looking out for my welfare. That was the perception he wanted me to have and the mentality he wanted me to embrace. The world was ours, my daddy always said, and it was because of him, this man, my dad, my hero why I was able to have a piece of this world.

Finally, my dad felt comfortable enough to let me in on the job David was doing. He had to do an exchange for almost a million dollars and he had promised David half. This was news I wanted to hear. David apparently didn't want to do it because he had heard through a third party that some police were setting up the entire deal, but my dad wasn't buying it and neither was I. David was just making the entire thing up just to get out of doing it. I don't know why he would give up the chance to make a half a million dollars. I found that rather strange. But I knew I wasn't going to let him even consider backing out. After much planning with my dad, I decided to drive David to the exchange because he was still fidgety and terrified about something possibly going wrong.

The transaction was scheduled at 9 p.m. on a Friday night. When David arrived at my house, he was shaking like it was 10 degrees outside. His eyes were wild and his fingers struggled to keep in order. It took me more than a minute to calm him down. I kept reminding him to stay focused...follow the money, and allow money to be his motivation. Obviously, it wasn't seeping through. He was too busy trying to change my mind, but all I could think about was that million dollars. I'd do anything to have a million dollars. I wanted to experience what being a millionaire felt like, looked like and smelled like. So many things flooded my mind...what's the first thing I'd do? I was getting too excited and there was nothing David could say to make me think or do otherwise.

David was unusually quiet the entire journey. He didn't even turn to look at me. After two hours of driving around, we finally reached an old abandoned house. There were no lights on, no signs of life and the grass at the side were parched and unkempt. Knowing my daddy, there was no way he would be caught dead in a place like this. Immediately, it dawned on me...this was the transaction zone. This was the secretive "trap house" far from civilization, onto a dingy path that led to almost nowhere. This was strictly business! The night was dark and now I was becoming nervous about what was about to go down. And, to make matters worse, David seemed to be acting strange. It was an unsettling feeling. Something wasn't sitting well with me anymore. He kept on wringing his hands as he sweated profusely. I swore I heard his heart pounding as if it were beating outside his damn chest. Well, who wouldn't? The damn place was dark and eerie. A shuffling in the bush quickly distracted us, only to see two squirrels dashing along the light pole. But amidst the frightening, scary house and the nauseous feeling, my mom's words kept echoing over and over: "Look past the money, Mo, and then you will see." I realized for the first time that money had become more important to me than my own life and my relationship with David. I loved it more than anything.

We got out of the car and walked closer to the door. Hairless, hungry cats roamed, meowing frighteningly in a bass-like cry. I had never heard such strange cat sounds before; they must be on drugs. The smell of stale pee and cat poop filled the air. I wanted to vomit. But "follow the money, Mo," so, I kept going. I knocked on the door first. Nothing. After about three loud bangs, I turned to look at David, and there they were, flashing lights and blasting sirens disrupted the silence of the night. The cats scurried in every direction. My eyes bulged and my breathing almost stopped.

Police swarmed the house. This had to be a scene from a movie or some fucking reality show that I didn't know about. There was no way this could be real. David had set my dad and me up. He looked at me with guilt. "Mo, I'm sorry. I'm so sorry...it wasn't me. It was you. You were just too Money-Hungry, Monique."

He was exactly right and, finally, I had to look past the money.

Dear Monique,

I get it. I really do, and, I understand the hustle. Money is power! Money makes you important and it's very important to have. We all want money...it makes us feel good. We feel complete with money; however, it's not the answer to all your problems and, get this, it certainly won't make your pain go away! While it is imperative to have, it's not the most important thing in the world.

If you have a man that loves you unconditionally, sometimes no money in the world can amount to that. If a man isn't buying you luxuries and diamonds all the time, it doesn't make him less of a man. Look at his potential. Focus on what he's trying to do for you and be content with the assurance that, with or without money, you still love him. Lest you forget, just like he has it today, tomorrow it can be gone. A man should be the protector and provider for his family but, remember, he is not obligated to spend money on you and it's definitely never worth him jeopardizing his life just to make sure you have a pair of Red

Bottoms. Support him through the good and the bad whether he

has 1,000 dollars in his savings or 10,000 dollars.

Remember, money can be shredded, spent or used over

and over again, but the true love of a good man is irreplaceable.

Don't worry about what's in his money clip, worry about the love

he has clipped in his heart.

Sincerely,

Juliet C.

Carmen, the Cuddle Buddy

The moment you realize you want to spend eternity with someone special, you pray that that forever begins tomorrow. I loved John. I was really in love with him. We had been together for almost two years and I was impatiently waiting for him to pop the question, yet I didn't want to rush him, so I left him alone until he was ready. It felt like forever and I really wanted to add the "r" between my little Ms. This "Miss" title I was carrying around for too long; it was time for a change. He was a lawyer and I had completed nursing school last fall. We were perfect for each other.

We purchased our first home in the spring and were really excited about the prospects of our future. We were both doing extremely well and had great careers. We were living the American dream, prosperous and successful. All that was missing was our kids, the white picket fence, two dogs and an official marriage license. I was ready for it to start now!

Every now and again I would throw him hints here and there about making me his wife, but I didn't want to be an asshole and annoy him about the same thing over and over again everyday and constantly hound him about giving me a ring. I think a man should do it when he feels like it and that a woman shouldn't have to beg or ask for it. He knew how bad I wanted to be married, so it was his job to just do it. My birthday was in exactly 13 days and I was hoping that it would just happen already!

I was turning the big 30 and nothing would excite me more than to be engaged to the man of my dreams. All the wedding plans had already been written and finalized in my head, so it was time to put these on paper and start the actual plans. Only time would tell how soon that would be.

After a long, hectic day of dealing with the cutest little "preemies" in the neo-natal intensive care unit, I was exhausted. Smeared in baby poop, baby spit-up saliva and the typical combination of milk and baby powder, I'd take a five-minute break to rest my weary feet and admire the tiny and most profound blessings ever bestowed on a human being...the gift of new life...a baby! And it was all in a day's work.

I sniffed the aroma and smiled. This was my life, taking care of babies. I loved it! It was all worth it for the 12 hours I spent inhaling poop, listening to the soft, innocent gurgling and chuckling, and cuddling and assuring the most innocuous and innocent lives that everything was "gonna be alright."

Then, there were moments when my mind drifted. I was in my bedroom, not the NICU. The lights were dim, I was rocking the baby and quietly humming to a soft lullaby played in the corner of the room. The crib was beautifully embellished and colorful decorations suspended from the ceiling. Only thing was, this baby was being breast-fed, suckling the last morsel of milk from its mother's breasts. This baby had John's eyes and our complexion. This baby was ours...mine and John's!

I walked into the house and followed my routine. I checked the mail, kicked off my shoes, ordered a pizza and headed for the tub. I knew I was wifey material; I didn't need anyone to confirm that or to remind me. But cooking every night was not my thing. That, however, didn't minimize my wifey qualities and status, and, besides, John had no problem with that. We both had hectic schedules and, so, he fully understood my situation. He was aware that some nights--well, most nights-- would end with a medium pizza or Chinese food. Well, probably after I get the ring I would make the kitchen my priority, purchase less frozen foods   and use the microwave less. I'm no Hercules, he accepted me for who I am and that's all that mattered. I'd endeavor to cook more, though, just to please my man. Well, we'd see.

I didn't even feel like going to the gym today like usual. I just wanted to relax and enjoy my last days of the 20s. I'd be 30 in a few weeks.

After my pizza, I showered and headed for the sheets. I wrapped myself tightly in the blanket and was watching Lifetime, my all-time favorite channel. It was pouring hard outside and the heavy drops were pushing against the window. I had just taken a hot, long, bubble bath and gulped down the last of the wine. My body was screaming for sleep and I was answering.

Scented oil lubricated every inch of my body from head to toe. Then I topped it off with a delicately fragranced nocturnal essence, a captivating aroma that would arrest you from a distance. I opened the window to let in a view of the panoramic beauty as I stood there enamored by the backyard of our beautiful home from the window. The tall palm trees were dancing in the calm winds as the almost withered leaves fell in droves from the huge oak burrowed deep in the earth along the pond. Then, I looked up to the skies just in time to witness a gorgeous rainbow creating a most magnificent silhouette across the eastern skies. What a divine sight! Well, well...this was our backyard!

Seemed like the perfect time to make sweet, passionate love to my fiancé--except for one thing, I didn't really have a fiancé. So, all that was left for me to do was to hug my pillow, drool on some fantasies and continue to stare at the television screen.

A few hours later, John entered the bedroom and planted a wet kiss on my cheek. We talked about our day and then he headed for the shower. I knew he wanted to relieve some tension after talking about his work day, so perhaps his intention was to release this during intercourse. He complained about being backed up because he hadn't had sex in about 27 days; as a result, he was sexually repressed and just wanted to explode. Somehow he was counting down the days to have sex. I don't know why but I thought it was pretty pathetic. I didn't feel like engaging in this argument about sex again, so I told him to lie next to me. Together we cuddled and wrapped ourselves inside the blanket while he slowly gnawed at my neck. He knew very well how that always turned me on, as my neck was my "weak" spot; however, I still didn't feel like having sex tonight--or any other night for that matter.

He continued kissing and then I felt his hands inching their way across my thighs and toward my crotch. I pretended not to notice but he eventually managed to slip his fingers inside my undies. I pushed the stop bottom. Why couldn't he just hold me? I grabbed his arm and wrapped it around my waist, pointing toward the television encouraging him to watch it with me.

"I don't feel like cuddling tonight, Carmen," he said, with a look of frustration and mild defiance with every word he spoke. And so I followed suit. With an equally frustrated countenance I snapped unapologetically, "And I don't feel like having sex every night, John."

We started arguing about how I never ever felt like having sex. It was a bit exaggerated on his part but there was also some truth in it. I admit, I love cuddling. I wasn't really a sex person; I would rather lie in my man's arms with my panties on some nights and not always have to think about having sex. Everything doesn't have to be sex; there are many other things couples can do to enjoy each other. John was too aggressive and a bit of a hound dog and that attitude was turning me off a bit. Just like I wasn't begging or harassing him for a ring, in the same way he shouldn't be begging me to have sex. I told him he needed to let it flow just like I was letting that proposal flow. He was upset with my comments and told me that there was no comparison. Oh, well, I didn't regret anything I said because in my opinion there was a comparison. The whole analogy was as simple as ABC: no ring, no sex. Period.

I didn't want to hear anything about him having blue balls again. Well, look at it this way: Maybe if he married me he would get all the sex he needs and he wouldn't have to complain about his balls. But, for now, he will have to settle with those blue balls. As you make your bed, you lie in it. I will not continue to play "wife." If I was good enough to have sex with every day, good enough to buy a home with, share a bank account with and enjoy all the trappings of a successful, happily married couple, then why couldn't I be a wife? Why couldn't we be official?

He didn't like the marriage talk at all; he resented it so much that he would get up and walk off on me, just like a zombie, leaving me talking to the television. I wanted to scream and tell him how I wish his balls would hurt till he died. But I couldn't. It wouldn't be true. God knows I loved this man. And right there on the sofa downstairs he would retire while I lay cuddled alone in my room watching TV. I was fine with it!

The next nine days went by with him and I on a touch-and- go, hi- and- bye schedule. Seldom did he speak and neither did I. He was trying to beat me mad but I was way ahead of his game. I'd been pretty darn upset for a while about him taking me for granted and not thinking I was good enough for a ring.

Tomorrow was my 30th birthday and I wasn't expecting anything at all. Especially not the two-carat diamond ring that I had picked out well over a year ago for a wedding that I had been planning since I was 10 years old! I knew he wasn't going to do anything special because he held on to grudges and, besides, he was still pretty upset about what had happened the other night.

So, I went ahead and chopped it up as a birthday with me, a movie, some Chinese food and a bottle of red wine.

On my way home from work I ordered my Chinese food and hoped that the delivery would beat me to the door. This birthday girl was hungry and was OK with celebrating alone. This was nothing strange.

As I walked into the house, I noticed that all the lights were turned off completely. I found that strange. John usually always leaves the oven light on, which was visible from the entrance, so I was becoming a bit uneasy as to this weird occurrence. I drew closer and heard a feint shuffle. I was about to make a b-line for the door when a deafening "SURPRISE!" erupted from the living room. And there they were, all excited.

John had invited a few of my friends, my parents and my sisters over for my birthday. Within a few minutes, what was an ordinary birthday surprise turned out to be an unbelievably special moment for me. Apparently, he had gotten over his feelings and realized that I was right. I was about to express my gratitude for such a wonderful and thoughtful gesture when John dropped to one knee. I thought he was tying his shoe lace but realized that he was clutching a small square object between his thumb and index fingers. My heart almost stopped beating. The moment I was waiting for all my life somehow started to feel awkward. It looked exciting but it didn't feel right. Maybe it was my nerves. Down on his knee, he opened a little black box with a ring. It was the ring! The same one I had shown him in the store. He swallowed, then he spoke, "Carmen, I know that you have been waiting for this and I almost felt like you gave me an ultimatum and, so, I wanted to ask you, in front of your family, friends and all the people that you love...Will you?"

"YES!" I screamed. "Yes! Yes! Yes!" He didn't have to ask me twice. I shouted yes before he could even finish the sentence. I was too excited to let him finish. But there was one thing missing, the audience compliments and well wishes. It was an almost surreal moment when John calmed me down, and with an uncanny look on his face, he patted me on the shoulder and demanded that I relax. Why was he stopping me? Everyone appeared confused and shocked. Maybe he did finish the question and I didn't hear him. Why didn't anyone else in the room look excited? I wondered. He was still in a stooping position when I asked him, "Wait, what, what did you ask me?"

"I said, will you be my cuddle buddy? Because obviously you don't want to be anything else." He slammed the ring box down, got off his knee and said, "Let me know when you're ready to be a wife and more than just a cuddle buddy."

Dear Carmen,

What can be compared to a warm, nice cuddle? Nothing! Lying in your bed, cozy in the sheets and wrapped snugly in your man's arms. Night after night can get pretty boring, so be prepared to be flexible and ingenious. Unlock the chains between your legs and allow your man to do more than just cuddle.

Sex doesn't have to be a daily occurrence, but we all have sexual gratifications that must be satisfied. Good old cuddling will not satisfy that sexual craving. You don't want your man looking for it somewhere else when you have it right between your thighs!

So, tired you may be. Go ahead and sip a little wine, turn the music on, dim the lights and ignite the fire between the sheets!

Sincerely,

Juliet C.

Kindhearted Keisha

I woke up with my favorite Bible verse echoing in my head. Ephesians 4: 32 ...Praises be to the Almighty. "Be kind to one another, tenderhearted, forgiving one another, as God in Christ forgave you." I parted the curtains to welcome a burst of sunlight; I was ready for the day. My praise music was on blast. I didn't want to wake up Phillip, so I lowered the volume and kept humming, "hmm um hmm um hmm hmm oh, yes, yesss---!"

"Keish, please, not today man, get up and get me some breakfast." Philip woke up grudgingly. He hated when I sing. According to him, it reminded him of a freezing cat screaming. I apologized for disturbing him and quickly shut the blinds so he could get a little more rest. After fluffing his pillow I hurried downstairs and headed for the kitchen.

I scrambled his eggs just as how he likes them, yellow, with a little brown around the edges and a dash of salt and pepper in the middle. I sprinkled the right amount this time. I didn't want him flipping it over again and cursing me out. My aim was to always please my man.

I had seasoned the steak the night before because I wanted to make sure it was just right: tender, juicy steak, just how he liked it, well seasoned and marinated for at least 12 hours prior to cooking. He was picky about his food and I wanted him to be satisfied before he left for a hard day's work. I flipped his pancakes and made sure the flour was perfectly circled and they were completely cooked, just how he liked them. Not too soft and not too stiff, kind of half way between.

Everything was done...cooked to perfection. His plate was prepared first and laid on the table, silverware perfectly positioned and matching, embroidered doilies to wipe his mouth. Freshly squeezed orange juice was poured into crystal glass and placed right beside his plate. This layout was fit only for a king and this was my king! He drank his orange juice fresh, so I woke up early to pick the choicest oranges from the tree; thankfully, the birds didn't attack them, so a few were still hanging. Very soon he would be bursting through the kitchen to clean up his favorite meal as the aroma was too much to bear. Then, the dreadful part was the eating and complaining. This too soft, that too crispy, too much salt here and there. Lord knows I hoped it was perfect for him and that he wouldn't have any complaints. Usually, when he doesn't like his breakfast, he throws it out and makes me cook him something else. I complied because I hated getting him all riled up in the mornings.

"Good morning, Phil." I didn't expect him to answer me back because he wasn't a morning person. While he was eating I tried to stay busy. I slowly pulled the iron and ironing board out of the linen closet and began to press his uniform. "You want to do that a little bit quieter? Damn, don't you see I'm trying to eat my food? Where's the respect?" he raised his voice angrily.

I tried to avoid any eye contact but I admit...I was pissed...and I could see that an argument was brewing. I needed a new ironing board, so I could only blame myself for his agitation. Phil hated that squeaky noise and he was right. He deserved to enjoy his meal undisturbed. So, I made sure to iron his uniform as quietly and neatly as possible, no crinkles, pay attention to all the details, making sure every crease was nice and straight. He had complained that a few days ago I sent him to work all wrinkled up and he didn't appreciate that, so this time, I checked every area to avoid any such recurrence.

"Get me some syrup!" he demanded. I wanted to say, "Get your lazy ass up and get your own dam syrup!" But I refused to answer back with anything rude. He didn't have to talk to me like I was his child. Then I thought, "What would Jesus do?" Not sure if Jesus would have kept his tongue, but I chose the high road; I watched my mouth. My mom always told me, "Be slow to speak and guard your tongue, for a kindhearted person is the woman that God loves the most." Essentially, that's what I was aiming to be. The woman that God loves most. It would have been nice if I could get Philip to love me like Christ did but I accepted that he was just hard to please and not everyone had that sweet, loving and patient spirit like I did. I was put on this earth to spread love and I hoped that one day he would eventually absorb all that I was aspiring to be and, by extension, wanted him to be.

A man likes a woman that doesn't have too much of a backbone because they need to be able to break them. Well, for Phillip, he was breaking me. I was already broken; all I knew how to do was pray. Pray for my marriage, pray that he would be more loving and appreciative and that he would give me the same admiration, love and respect that I gave to him.

I spent many hours on my knees, praying that this man would stop taking my love for granted. It didn't matter if the food was crafted by a top chef, he'd still find a reason to complain, if his clothes were starched like the cleaners, there would still be a wrinkle, and if I crept through the house like a mouse, he would still hear noise. I was convinced he was just a mean-spirited person. I kept my anointing oil whenever I felt a disagreement starting. I would flicker a little around the corners of the house and cast those demonic spirits away. It didn't help, but I knew

God would soon send me the peace I desperately yearned for. Some men were just hard to please, I guess, and he was definitely that man.

The friends he allowed me to have would always tell me, "A man will only do what you allow them to do. If you don't set limits, they will take advantage." So, what was I allowing that was wrong? Not speaking to him disparagingly or arguing back with him was wrong? I was doing right with my man by keeping peace in my home. He was the head and I was the tail, so I made sure to follow the teachings of the Bible and do what he needed me to do as a wife. It's not that I was allowing him to mistreat me but at the same time he was my voice and whatever he said...goes. I know that I no longer had an opinion in my marriage but the woman I was is the woman Phil allowed me to become. I wanted to listen to him because I was no longer valid and my thoughts didn't make as much sense as his did. He told me what to wear, how to do my hair...everything I did was to please him. I ate what he instructed me to eat, went where he told me to go (which was really nowhere) and I did what he told me to do. He had become my master.

I tried to enjoy life instead of staying at home all the time cooking, cleaning and taking care of my husband, but he didn't like me going out. He would say he didn't want folks getting in my head and turning me against him. The only place he really allowed me to go was church, and sometimes he was even skeptical about that. He warned me not to get too close to the pastor or any of the church brothers, and to be careful how much money I put in my envelope for my tithes. I usually hide my tithes and offerings as he didn't allow me to drop anything over 10 dollars. I'd ask him on Sundays to accompany me and get a word from the pastor but he would tell me that he too has a word for the pastor, and it's not a nice word. After a while I got tired of his criticisms and negative behavior toward the church, so I just left him alone.

After finishing his breakfast, he got dressed and left for work. Honestly, I enjoyed when he went to work because I was able to relax in my peaceful zone, enjoy the house alone without having to worry unnecessarily about the flaws he found and his usual nagging complaints. He made me feel inadequate and incomplete, or I should say insecure. I was always scared about annoying him. No matter how much I tried, he would still find something to antagonize me about. So, I turned my praise music back up and began my house duties. The house was super clean before he came home because I didn't work. Perhaps that's the least I could do to ensure that he was contented. I did my part. He said women were worthless creatures and that their only place was in the kitchen and the bedroom, so he never bothered me much about getting a real job.

I walked from the laundry room and was about to iron his drawers and socks when I realized I had six missed calls from Phillip. He was taking time from his work day to call me from his job and, as usual, it wasn't for any afternoon loving. He had a bone to pick, and I was about to be shredded into a million pieces. I prayed before returning his calls because six calls meant that I was in hot water, and I wasn't ready for the fiery death I was about to receive. It rang twice. He answered aggressively, just like I anticipated and began his rant. "You are so stupid, Keisha. I'm so sick of having to remind you about every little thing!" I moved the phone away from my ear because he was about to destroy my eardrum. I was confused because I'm sure that I had crossed all my Ts. I went through his lunch bag at least 10 times before zipping it up. What in the world did I forget? He continued, "I feel like you are just the dumbest ass woman in the world!" he screamed.

By now I was really wondering what he was talking about. I could no longer hold my tongue. "Phil, what did I for---" He cut me off and reminded me, "Speak when spoken to!" I got quiet. I was fussing in my head but I had to respect him, so I allowed him to continue. "I can't believe you forgot. When I get home, I am going to make sure you remember. Make sure you have my dinner ready!" He screamed even louder and then bang! He hung up, just like that.

I took a break from cleaning the house and tried to remember what I forgot. Then, it hit me. I forgot to pack his banana. He called me six times, cursed me out and went off on me because I forgot his fruit, a little yellow banana. It was unbelievably ridiculous, but to him, it wasn't. He was very petty like that, so I was not the least bit surprised that he was starting a war over a missing banana. I wanted to curse, but I thought again, "What would Jesus do?" So, I grabbed the mop and continued humming and cleaning so that I could get dinner started. I read the text he sent. For dinner he wanted "A whole chicken, stuffed with peppers and Italian onions (where was I going to get Italian onions?) seasoned with a pinch of lemon supreme." I bet he wanted me to go out and kill the chicken, too! Finely cut ribs ("Make sure they're no bigger than eight inches and no smaller than six") coated with homemade, tangy BBQ icing, jalapeño gizzards floating over a bed of rice with chive butter onion sauce and a fresh wild caught salmon drizzled with honey bourbon dip." I didn't even bother to look at the dessert he wanted. The last time he had requested a four-layer cake so that he could take it for the people at his job. I wasn't his chef but like I said, I wanted to keep the peace and if that's what he wanted, I had to get started.

On my way to the grocery store, I stopped by his job to deliver his banana. I texted him that I was outside and within minutes he appeared with a beastly attitude, grabbed his banana, shook his head and, after staring me sternly in the eyes, he rebuked, "Don't let this happen again, you hear me?" Repeating it twice. Then, he turned away and disappeared inside the building. Not even "Hi" or "Thank you." Well, I'm not surprised. What would Jesus do?

I know he was still pretty mad and was probably wondering whether I had cooked what he had asked for. Well, in our world, saying "no" was not an option, so it's not about me nor how I felt, it was all about him, hence his wish was always my command. His lavish meal was ready. I was relying on the fact that he was usually more docile and calmer in the evenings. I would usually leave his food in the microwave with a note and Scripture while I was at Bible study. Sometimes I'd see the note and Scripture covered with food or ripped and thrown in the trash. I never asked if he liked it or not but I figured maybe something written on it was something he liked. While it wasn't customary for him to thank me for the dinner, he wouldn't argue with me when I got home either, so at least I was happy about that, no fuss, no complaints. This made me feel hopeful and appreciative of him, and that I had accomplished something great for the day. Most nights ended with him on top of me, bucking and hunching me like an animal. I was an unwilling participant because he forced me into doing certain acts against my will that made me feel very violated. But perhaps it was my job to please him in spite of how he treated me. Guess I had to go with the flow. It's just what Jesus would want me to do.

I drove away from his work place, stopped by the grocery store and then headed home. Before I started dinner, I crouched in my prayer closet and began praying for peace in my home. And then something spoke to me. I don't know if it was God or what but something spoke to me. I dutifully prepared his meal, got dressed for church, and left my note and Scripture in the microwave. I would leave him a Scripture from the Book of Psalms, but tonight, it was a different message. It was a new verse on an empty playlet. It read: "I'm not your slave, your maid nor your chef. I'm your wife. I kept asking myself what would Jesus do...and Jesus answered. This is what He said: 'Do unto others as you would have them do unto you!' I deserve better! I deserve to be with someone better than an arrogant, no good, foul-mouthed, ungrateful, unappreciative asshole like yourself!

So, instead of enjoying your dinner, you can take a bite of this, you evil piece of shit!"

With all my love,

Kindhearted Keisha: Verse one, Chapter... DONE!!!

Dear Keisha,

Being a sweetheart is all good and great, but not if it means letting someone walk all over you and break your heart. I agree that women should be slow to speak and quick to forgive, but that forgive part is what qualifies us to be so subservient and gullible. This is why men take advantage and continue to have multiple extra-marital affairs.

Listen, know when enough is enough and always have a level of respect for a man, but that doesn't necessarily mean that you have to be indifferent or oblivious to all his wrongdoings so as to avoid conflicts. It's OK to have an opinion. Your feelings are valid and should be valued. Brushing them aside to please your man isn't healthy or fair to you or the relationship on a whole. One thing is for sure: If you want to be a great woman to your man or your kids, you have to start with you...it begins with you. If you don't have yourself together, then it will be difficult to take care of your man or your kids.

So, you can be sweet and loving but that doesn't mean you have to be complicit to your own demise and allow others to trample you. So, it's important to get yourself in order first, then the rest will fall into place. Get a backbone and remember it's OK to say no. It's OK to have an opinion and put your foot down.

And if you can't get the respect you want, demand the respect you need. And, failing all the above, that relationship or that man is not your cup of tea!

Sincerely,

Juliet C.

Freaky Felicia

Last weekend I finally mustered the courage to open up to Anthony, something I have been wanting to do for a long time. There was a lot on my mind and so much I wanted to tell him, but I was waiting for the right moment, the right time. My big problem was me and Anthony's sex sessions. I demanded to know why his sex drive had been so low during our relationship. I might not have had a lot of experience, but, from the little I knew, I was able to figure out that something wasn't quite right with him in the bedroom. I wanted to find out why he never seems to be into me like that. Having lame sex bothered me a whole lot. In fact, it made me feel terrible, like something was wrong with me down there. It's like I was desperate to please him so badly, to go all the way out to make him happy, but I don't think he ever enjoys it.

I can't help if I've never learned the basic sex tricks and skills. I grew up kind of sheltered and wasn't into sex like that. I wasn't sure if I was supposed to mount him and ride him like a horse, or lie gently on my back and just spread my legs. My body is already programmed to the missionary style, so to expect anything else from me, was just asking for too much. Ridiculous! But I was willing to try, anyway. Anything to please my man. I just couldn't understand why, after so many years, he hadn't gotten use to my sex, though. I guess no matter how long you've been with someone, every now and then you've got to spice it up!

Anthony thinks I'm old-fashioned and boring for not wanting to put a dick in my mouth. Sucking on a nasty, slimy dick? No way! A dick is made to go into the vagina and not down my damn throat! Our sex had become so routine to the point that I knew exactly how long it would last, what groans he would make, and even what the rhythm and beat would be. Most times I would catch him watching the TV while we're doing it or playing on his phone. I'm not even sure if that should upset me. Am I that boring that he has to be watching the television? Maybe I am cause I don't like it doggy style at all. It reminds me too much of two damn dogs! Doing it from the side makes me feel awkward and getting on top just isn't going to happen. He is always one to be very open to me, so I could no longer bite my tongue about it. So, here it is, I really think the time had come for me to be straight forward with him. After about 13 minutes of sex--no eye contact, no chemistry, no interaction, it was just too much. I pushed him off of me, pulled the sheet to hide my nakedness, stared him dead in the eyes and asked, "Anthony, what's the problem? Do I not please you enough, are you having sex with someone else or is it just not good?"

Without any hesitation, he looked me straight in the face and replied, "Baby, it's just not good." He didn't even stutter. A bold, cold, straight forward answer. Wow! Even though I wanted the truth, damn, his honesty took me by surprise. It was how he said it, though.

Well, I just have to suck it up and handle it. I asked for it, didn't I? I just couldn't believe he could've been so blatant and brave to spit it out just like that. I didn't want to lose my man because I couldn't please him and there was no questioning whether I had some good pussy down there. I just needed to know how to use it to the best of my advantage. But what was I to do? Compromise my comfort level just so he could get the fuck of his dreams? Our five-year anniversary was approaching and I just knew I had to make this right. So, I went online and looked up every possible thing I could do to please my man. I searched every porn site, dug through old magazines and interviewed a few of my friends about what good sex was. Damn, I had to get this right! Something had to give and I would do anything to make this a night he'd never forget. Four hundred and ninety-seven dollars! That was my fucking bill from Extreme Pleasure Freak Sex Store. I don't even know what could have cost so much to have that kind of bill near 500 dollars. I looked back over my checklist one last time just to make sure I had everything that I needed to make tonight really special. Vibrators, anal rings, cock rings, butt plugs, ass gel, pussy lollipop, throat tranquilizer, anal beads, you name it, I had it! Damn my shit was on point!

Then, it hit me. Should I get the dominatrix outfit and a

whip? Or would I be going too far? Hell, I put it in the cart anyway and swiped my debit card. I had nothing to lose, I must admit, though, I've never done anything like this before, so I was a bit embarrassed. As I approached the cashier, I was doing everything to cause a distraction. From scrolling on my phone, to digging my nose and twisting my hair, I was a bit uncomfortable. A woman buying three big black 10-inch dildos was before me and I was so glad that she didn't pay any attention to my cart. The cashier seems accustomed to people, no matter their appearance, buying just about anything. This was her job. I stood there admiring all her piercings and enquired about the pain. She explained to me that most men she dealt with admired her piercings and told her they were sexy so, as you can imagine, I quickly paid for all my heavenly merchandise and followed her toward the back where they do piercings and tattoos. I was ready, so ready to do anything to please my man! What should I get? A tongue ring, nose ring, navel ring, vagina ring? The hell...I wanted them all! I wondered which one Anthony would think was more hot, sexy and spicy.

Well, only time would tell.

Dinner was just a few hours away and this girl was leaving no stones unturned. So, after about two well-spent hours in the sex store, I felt well prepared and fully armed for the night's events. I was ready to celebrate my anniversary. It was going down tonight! I made a promise and I was going to fulfill it. Tonight would be the last night that he would label me as boring and lousy. My mama ain't raise no fool and I knew better than to be having boring sex. Boy, did I have a surprise for him!

Dinner reservations were for 7 p.m. I was ready. My perfume was dotted on every ounce of my starving body while my 20-inch Candy Jewels Luxury Malaysian hair swept across my shoulder and punctuated my matching shoes, **which** went beautifully with my two-piece bodycon skirt set. I didn't overdo it because I was saving the element of surprise for a little later. His cologne...that cologne... immediately I was like a super soaker water gun. Obviously, the KY jelly that the lady at the store suggested was really doing its job. The car seat was drenched! My nipples grew hard and even the nipple rings were erect. Yes, I decided to pierce my nipples. Anthony began driving and I started kissing him all over his shoulder and neck. I didn't want to distract him but I couldn't help myself. His dick bulged from those fitted jeans. His eyes went wide and he asked me if I was OK. I didn't speak. Well, I couldn't speak! This very moment my tongue was doing all the talking. There was no time for silly conversation. The car swerved a little but I couldn't afford to be distracted and, really, I didn't care. My plan was in effect and it was working. I put my nerves aside as I was determined to show him what I was working with tonight. No more little Miss Simple Sally! Then, as he gained his composure at the wheel, he appeared a bit surprised of my actions. I was hoping that he wasn't thinking that I was about to kill him, so I stuck out my tongue seductively, rubbed his throbbing dick, and gently stuck my hands inside his shirt and then started playing with his nipples. His dick was hard as a brick. I guess this was the first time I was really noticing his manhood. My hands caressed his lower body, and he moaned. Then, as I moved down lower, the moans grew more intense and his foot pressed a little harder on the accelerator. I don't know if it was him or me who pulled the dick out first, but before I knew it, it was lying on his thigh, rock hard, staring hard at me. I knew his dick wasn't going to suck itself so, as soon as we locked eyes, I took a deep, deep, breath, swallowed hard, reached down and went to work. For once in my life I wasn't scared. I had prepared too much for this occasion, so I was ready to suck till that dick was limp. This was my first time and, honestly, it felt really good.

At this point, driving while being sucked up was proving to be too dangerous so, he decided to pull over. I figured I must have been doing a damn good job from his loud and continuous moans and groans of "ooohs and ahhhs." I was steadfast in my dick sucking. I licked, I slurped and I sucked. Tonight I made my dick-sucking debut! Hold the applause! I was happy he stopped the car because it allowed me to lower his pants enough to get to his glistening balls. I wanted to suck those first. I was following instructions on the porn video I saw the night before. And it was really working. I stuck to the script that I had memorized. I left out no detail. So, based on the directions, I started with the balls. I juggled them in my mouth, almost choking, I slurped and he trembled and meowed like a damn cat. The more I sucked, the more horny I became and he did, too. He was making some weird sounds that seemed unhuman. But I wasn't scared. It felt like I had two sweet and sour jaw breakers in my mouth. And, baby, those were the two best jaw breakers I ever sucked. I loved how it felt and I was ready to suck the skin off his dick. He must have had seafood earlier because I'm sure I tasted curried lobster tails in his cum as he squirted about two ounces down my throat. Where the fuck did he get lobster tails from? Anyway! Damn, the flavor was all over my mouth. I swirled it around my tongue, trying to trap and savor all the juices. And, yes, I swallowed. The thick, creamy texture slithered down the back of my throat like mayo! It was divine! "Ohhh, baby, baby, don't stop!" he begged . Well, just to let you know, I was just getting started. I knew that this great performance would guarantee us both another five years, and tonight I was pulling out all the stops!

He couldn't believe that I was giving him head in his car and neither could I. Then, the moment I was waiting for.... He started tickling and caressing my legs with his cold hands, until they became warmer. Then, he started working the fingers. The first finger felt like I was going to explode. I know my sweet juices turned him on since he had never felt me so wet before, and the fact that I wasn't wearing panties made him even hotter. All I could hear him say was, "Damn baby, damn! You are a beast tonight. Shit!" I liked how he screamed my name while he finger-fucked my pussy, probing and thrusting, driving me insane...all the way to the restaurant.

At the table, we decided to sit next to each other instead of our usual across-the-table seating. This was a big change. We had let our guards down and were "sexually radicalized." I don't know if the waitress saw me jacking his dick under the table or heard him cum but, I hope she didn't, because, before the dinner even arrived, we were heading back home for a special dessert I had so lavishly prepared. There was no need to eat food or drink anything besides creamy cum and body juices. We had lots of fucking to make up for. Years of neglect were gonna be rolled into one night.

We entered the house and we couldn't wait! You could smell fuck from a distance. Sex was written in the air. I had him sit down on the couch as he waited for me to come out of the room. The pole was already set up in the living room and I crawled out seductively in my black dominatrix suit and a whip while Trey Songz "Slow Motion" played. I gyrated provocatively on the pole until I managed to unzip the pussy, nipple and ass crack of my suit. At first I felt weird, but it was an exciting kind of weird. I kept right on dancing as he cheered me on. I walked over to him slowly and sat on his face backward and sucked him again while he ate me out from behind. Finally, he ripped off my outfit and I handed him the whip as he slapped my ass back and forth. Suddenly, he reached for the anal beads I had laid on the table and worked them in my ass gently. The sensation was overwhelming pleasant as each bead glided and disappeared in my asshole. It felt good! My hungry ass was screaming for his big black dick. Then, as he licked my ass crack, I felt it plunging inside my vagina, slowly gliding in, then, a smooth thrust until every inch was all cushioned deeply inside. I swore I felt that dick all the way in my throat! He wasted no time in pumping me from behind, slapping and straddling me like a stallion as pleasurable screams and moans escaped my lips. He was tearing up and rear ending that pussy. I was in Heaven! It felt as though we had just met and fucking like we invented it. Finally, he and I were enjoying each other's sex for the first time in five damn years. This was proof that I was really missing out on good, hard-core fucking, and gave up years of pleasure for being so shy under the sheets.

After about six different positions, we were tired. I picked up my handcuffs and vibrator off the table and led him into the room for the ultimate surprise. As the door opened, I saw his bottom lip drop to the floor in shock. "Party of three, anyone?" I whispered in my sexy voice. Yes, tonight I was giving my baby the surprise of his life. A threesome. I led him over to our dessert, a beautiful friend of mine who was totally willing to join in our fun. She couldn't wait, so I decided to dive in first. Anthony could not believe what was happening as I begin eating her sweet pussy. He was breathing short and heavy, with disbelief written all over his face. Then, he looked at me as if I was crazy, tapped me on my shoulder and whispered, "Damn, baby, what's gotten into you tonight?" The question wasn't what, it was who and tonight I was "Freaky Felisha," that's who! No more Simple Felisha, I had my freaky side out and was ready to fuck the night away!

Dear Felicia,

Nothing is better than a freaky, fun and spontaneous relationship. It's important that you know what your man likes under the sheets, but you also have to make sure you feel comfortable with it. Sex is a beautiful thing and it is extremely crucial to the longevity and survival of a meaningful relationship.

Men get tired of the same old routines. Oh, how they love a woman role-playing, buying new lingerie, spraying on a new perfume and enjoying her man in the sheets. These are treats you give your man and they don't have to be done all the time. Be creative; be spontaneous. Don't be afraid to step outside the box, and don't be afraid to jump out of one either! Keep the fires lit, but don't burn the house down.

Sincerely,

Juliet C.

Laura the Label Whore

The first thing I noticed was the Rolls-Royce. I didn't know

if the driver was paralyzed, had one leg, one eye, no teeth or

crippled. I didn't care, really. All I knew is that it was a man behind

a Bentley and I was ready to see who was getting out of this ride. I

hurried to put Dior and Gucci in their car seats because I didn't

want him to see me with my kids. I know how that can be a big

turn–off to most men. I was looking my best. I was hot shit today.

I had spent all my rent money on the outfit I was sporting and it

was sure worth every dime. My neighborhood booster and best

friend Tim never failed me when it came to getting me the cutest

clothes. He did his weekly snatch and grab in all the latest

boutiques. Wearing my vintage Gucci bag, Gucci belt, my Red

Bottoms, boutique dress, Chanel shades, Chanel phone case, LV

finger nail designs and my Rolex watch--Tim knew my taste and

he knew exactly what I wanted, and he delivered. And today, he hooked your girl up. You couldn't tell me nothing! And even if you did, I didn't care because I knew I was looking like a million bucks.

Mr. Richard parked his Bentley right next to my Mercedes and quickly jumped out, showing off his Tom Ford suit. I was curious about the kind of job he had but, then again, I didn't care. I saw dollar signs and that's all that mattered. I slowly turned and walked to my trunk pretending to search for something, hoping that he'd notice my ass, breasts, lips or something...anything. Nothing caught his attention. He stayed on his phone as I listened in closely to his conversation. He was doing some kind of business transaction and it seemed he may have been an owner of some major corporation. JACKPOT! Oh, well, whatever I had to do, this man was going to pay me some attention today! Even If I had to flatten my car tires, trip, fall, scream, pretend I needed directions, or put on a fainting show...something must work to make him see me today! Period!

I curled my lip and pounced over to his car. "Sir, do you know where a mall is in the area? I'm not from around here and

I'm a little lost." I lied. And it seemed that I had finally caught his attention. Finally! Immediately, he hung up the phone and I could see him staring hard at my sexy lace Victoria Secret bra. My heart was thumping. "Nice bra," he said. We got into a small conversation and he began telling me all about the multi-million-dollar organic business he owned and operated. I couldn't hear anything he was saying because my eyes were locked onto his Movado watch, his spotless manicure and a glistening diamond rock on his finger. Was he married? Honestly, I didn't care about that either. He was a good catch and I was determined to bait his ass. Right before he and I could really feel each other out, I had to cut the conversation short because Dior started her whining in the backseat. I was hoping he didn't hear her. If only she would just shut up. I was hoping she didn't call me Mommy either.

"Is that your baby?" he questioned. "Oh, no! No! Those are my sisters' kids," I quickly responded.' Yep, I lied again. "I'm helping her out for the weekend." Now, don't get me wrong, I love my kids with all my heart but I didn't want to run the risk of missing out on this opportunity and mess up what could have been something special. I wasn't thinking long term with him anyway. For me, this was a grab and go situation. Get what I could get out of him and then keep it pushing. So, it's not like he's ever going to find out about my kids anyway. Men never do. I was just trying to get what I can get: a few bags, a couple pairs of shoes, some Brazilian hair, a car note paid and that's all. I was not looking for love, just material items. The only men I love were on bills and their names were Jackson, Grant and Franklin.

He handed me his business card and told me to give him a call if I was ever interested in company investing. Blah, blah, blah. I didn't want to hear about any of that. The only investment I was looking for was him investing in my shopping habit. Oh, yes, he had to be married because I didn't get the cell phone number; I got the business card instead. That was cool with me, though. But I wanted to know more about who he really was. I hurried home to light up Google to do my research on him. I couldn't wait to see exactly who he was. Maybe I could find his net worth or something. I needed to make sure he was who he appeared to be. I can smell fake from a million miles away. I had carried enough replica handbags and wore tons of replica shoes to know fake when I see it. But somehow this dude seemed legit. And so he was. I looked him up before I even got home. I know it's wrong to use my phone and drive, especially with my kids in the car, but I was so excited and curious at the same time I couldn't help myself. Check this: 46K followers on IG, pictures dining in fancy restaurants every other night, shopping in expensive stores, traveling first class to exotic destinations. Well, well, he was definitely who he said he was and I was about to be one lucky lady. I was kind of surprised when I didn't see any woman on his IG. I thought maybe he wasn't really into his wife or maybe he had a lot of side chicks. Truth is, I couldn't care less. I was trying to get the newest pair of Louboutins and he was going to be my new paymaster.

Richard King's Organic Corporation. I didn't want to appear too needy and thirsty, but truth is, I was needy and the thirst was real. I had to be careful not to expose my motive, though. I waited a little while before calling him. Better yet, I gave it some thought and decided to wait a few hours before giving him a call.

I hurried up and put some microwave dinner in for the kids because I couldn't cook and, even if I did know how to cook, I wasn't about to mess up my nails. In this house, Chef Boyardee and Ramen Noodles did all the cooking. After they ate, I tucked them in bed and waited for the sitter to get here with them. Then, I slid into my lavish Roberto Cavali bedroom. I had everything Cavali: sheets, pillows, pictures, rug, curtains, pictures and two lamps. Any man who slept between these sheets were sleeping in pure damn luxury. Hopefully, Richard could be that man tonight!

I sat on my bed holding my cell phone. An hour went by and I couldn't wait any longer, so I called his office. "Hi, Mr. King. This is Laura, whom you met in the parking lot today. I am wondering if you're available for dinner or...or something tonight. I'd like you to look at my investment portfolio that I feel will be beneficial and profitable for your company." The lies were just rolling off my tongue.

He hesitated. Embarrassing. Oh, my God, what was I thinking? Maybe I was moving too fast. "Mr. King...hello... Are you there?' Finally, he answered, "Laura...tonight will work. My driver and I will pick you up around 7:30." I hung up and took a long deep breath. This was my big night. A car pick me up? Yes, *Gawd*! This is the type of man I should have met years ago. Shit, if I'm lucky maybe I can get more than what I'm bargaining for.

I didn't really know how I was going to pull this portfolio deal off, but I needed a reason to get him to dinner. What was I going to wear? I knew I needed to call my friend Tim to see if he had anything sexy for me. I had to look *hawt* because when Richard first saw me in the parking lot he didn't seem all that interested in me at all, so tonight I had to let him see my body instead of talking about some damn investments. He would be out of his damn mind if he ever thought that I would waste this date talking about a damn boring portfolio. Finally, Tim came over with a few bags and choices of some sexy lingerie. He was excited

for me and I bragged to him that I had finally hit the jackpot and I

needed him to sell me his best. If you ever wanted any design,

Tim is whom you call. You could never go wrong shopping out of

his trunk he had the latest fashion with the best prices. If he

didn't have a penis, I'd say he and I were just alike. He reminded

me a lot of myself. We made a lot of jokes calling each other gold

diggers. I had to admit, though, he was better at getting all the

men with money, too. A few of my tricks I actually learned from

Tim. He met his jackpot a few months ago. He never gave me too

many details but I knew he had a man with a lot of money. He

would always refer to this good mysterious friend as Mr. Racks

because he was always giving Tim tons of racks. See, that's what I

was looking for, too. And tonight was gonna be my big break.

So, after rummaging through Tim's clothing assortment

with hopes of finding something that would really stand out, I

found it! A sequined Versace dress, hot off the racks. I needed a

sexy shoe and I found those, too. A pair of Manolo's I begged Tim to take off his feet and let me wear them for the night. Tim dressed better than me, so I knew I couldn't go wrong.

Seven thirty was approaching. The doorbell rang. I stood in the mirror fixing my bra and butt pads and asked Tim to let the driver know I would soon be out. I learned that you always have to keep a man waiting for you. Besides, everything had to be perfect and I needed to make sure I was looking my best. Damn, I hope I didn't have to give up the pussy tonight, but I was prepared for anything. Whatever meant me having a few bucks in my hand would be worth it tonight.

I rushed to the door with my plan in motion, smiling like a little child, eager for a warm, tight hug, only to hear Tim screaming and yelling. Oh, God, what the hell does Tim have going on out here already? I was nervous, hoping Tim wasn't embarrassing me. To my surprise, Tim and Richard were engaged in a full blown-out argument. "Is everything OK?" I asked curiously, shocked. Tim turned to me, rolling his eyes and batting his lashes. He stared at me fuming and sweating while pointing at

Richard. "Laura," he said boldly. "This is my man, Mr. Racks, I've been telling you about, and Richard, this is my friend Laura I told you all about. Please meet Laura, the Label Whore," he said, pointing at me.

I stood there, frozen, my heart beating outside my chest, my mouth wide opened and my stomach in my ass. So much for my big break tonight!

Dear Laura,

We all like to look pretty, both for ourselves and for our man.

But that does not necessarily mean that we have to go out of our way to get up only in expensive threads that are ordinarily out of our reach price-wise, forcing us to go over the top to get those designer duds.

Looking good doesn't have everything to do with designer labels. Looking good is about having a sense of style, about knowing about fashion and what looks good on you to wear. Men won't be wooed by that Versace label on the dress alone, but how good you looked on the date. So, the Versace label didn't get you the man—it was you with your sense of fashion that made the evening.

Don't let the dress wear you—you wear the dress, and that can be achieved not just with designer labels but off-the-rack clothes, too. So don't make your focus who you have to wear to look dolled up but on what you're wearing that makes you look like a million bucks.

Your man will appreciate just as well a package that's put together with the right choices from the mall's box stores than just the real expensive things that are out of your reach. Your obsession with just labels puts the focus on the clothes rather than on your man—and he may not care about the difference of who you're wearing but how you're wearing it that catches his eye.

Sincerely,

Juliet C.

Sydney, the Side Chick

It could be in an old dilapidated motel, on the backseat of his car or a quick meet up in a parking lot, anywhere we could get it in, we were going to get it, as long as I had the chance to see him. Even if it only lasted 30 minutes, we were getting it. When we were together, our love was like magic. Maybe because in the real world temporary fantasies don't last very long. The only difference was, I wanted this moment for a lifetime. Even though he had his wife at home, it meant nothing to me and it meant nothing to him. At least, that's how it felt. She might have his last name, but I had him last night and that was the only difference between the two of us. And, go ahead, if you must, and judge me, but the latter was more important to me. One way or the other, he was my man, too, and no little marriage certificate was going to make me feel otherwise.

I had given just as much of myself, or maybe even more, and I wasn't about to let that go for her sake. Truth is, he had already explained to me what the real situation was on the inside, assuring me that it wasn't as how it appeared on the outside. He told me that he only stuck around because they had a kid and she remained loyal all that time in spite of what was going on. Well, it didn't make sense that he wanted to cheat on his loyal wife, though.   See, I think it's just sad that the way you reward someone's loyalty and fidelity is by being disloyal. Oh, well, that was her dumb ass. If you can lie next to a man every night and not know that he's cheating on you, then, you're one simple jackass who is just as shallow and naive as I am. The wife always refers to the mistress as the side chick or side ho; in a sense it's good because I don't have to deal with the problems that "wives" do at home. I'm a side chick, and being a side chick means when you get him pissed, he comes straight to me. I'm his stress reliever, and I'm damn good at my job. I know his stay with me is short lived, but I cherish every minute he spends with me...and not her. Yeah, it hurts a little on the inside, but when you've become accustomed to doing it for so long, it becomes a part of you. It shapes your identity, essentially, it's just who you are, and this is me. You want more but because you know it's going to be too hard having all of a man, you take the piece you can, no matter how small, and you run with it. Of course, it weighs heavily on you at times, mentally, physically and spiritually, but you continue to be the little side piece because it's better than having no piece at all. You try and mask the hatred and jealousy you feel when you see him with his woman; traveling, laughing and being exclusive for the world to see. Then, you are forced to cover up that hurt inside, it is hard. It's even harder when you have to spend all the important holidays alone, like Christmas, Valentine's Day and other special holidays and precious moments that only lovers share. Those days can't be divided with a side piece, so you have to wait all of 24 hours (sometimes 48) to see him. Then, to add insult to injury, you can't post him in your pictures on social media, neither are you privy to even take a picture of him or with him because you both have a secretive relationship. When you know he's with his family, capturing memories that the two of you will never capture, that shit doesn't go down too well at all; it just doesn't feel good.

But I love this man. The way he makes me feel, it can't be fake. So, like I said before, I'll settle with a tiny bit than nothing at all. A little piece will grant me enough peace to continue living. The passion, the love making...his own woman obviously can't make him feel like me. Why me? Why did he chose me? I will never know. But I'm willing to ride this wave as long as I can. And, if that takes being number two, then so be it. Being number two only sucks in competition and he was already sneaking out to see me every night so, clearly, there was no competition between his wife and me. It's hard that I can't wake up to him in the mornings but I've learned to take the good with the bad and go with the flow.

Right now, it may seem like it's just sex, but we do have some chemistry. I'm almost sure that one day it's definitely going to be something more. I look forward to those days in particular when he has a temporary "break-up" with his wife. Then, I have him all to myself for at least 48 uninterrupted hours. Then, they're back together, and I'm left there like a fool…. waiting… and I'm still waiting. You see, he's been promising me he'd do this for a long time now and deep down I believe he just needs a little push. Well, tonight I was going to give him that push.

We pulled into the dark garage. He backed his car into a secluded area and stepped out of the vehicle. "I'll be right back, baby." Man, oh, man, I thought to myself. I love this man, I love him. Every time he opened his mouth I got butterflies. I know I shouldn't be feeling this way about someone else's man, but truth is, he was more my man than he was hers. But you couldn't help but love him. He was always doing something romantic and treating me like no man had ever treated me. So damn charming! I didn't care if he had a pointed nose and ebony skin, I had never ever felt so much love and appreciation from any man like the love I felt from Kevin. As soon as he returned to the car, he laid the receipt on the dash board, right in my view. Being nosy, I sat up to check out the price to see how much I was worth tonight.

Damn. Just $57.99 for three hours? It was cheap, but I didn't mind, still better than the usual $49.99. He loved taking me to one of those pay-by-the-hour hotel rooms and I wasn't going to complain at all. I was just too excited that he wanted to spend some quality time with me anyway. I liked this hotel a lot because it was so quiet and isolated. This was our moment, just he and I, lost in the secrecy of our heated romance. These were special moments where I could fantasize that they were forever. It was cozy, romantic and discretely tucked away from the maddening crowd. Exactly how he liked us to be. Here was a man who opened doors for me, gently held my arm and helped me alight his SUV in my six-inch heels. I had to look good for him, at whatever cost. I was willing to be a little uncomfortable even if it meant hurting me, but anything to please my man was my goal.

Once we were inside we walked into a grand hotel room where we were greeted by a welcoming ambience. There I stood, almost motionless, staring at the Italian vaulted ceilings, California king heart-shaped bed sprinkled with bright red and baby pink rose petals, and a majestic, mega-size, crescent-shaped jacuzzi in the center of the floor. This place was everything, and was much fancier than our usual spots. Well, thinking about $57.99 was no comparison. I couldn't believe it was so "cheap" with all its magnificence; truly, my mind was blown. Perhaps I just wasn't used to the finer things or had been downgraded to only decaying rooms, so it was kind of hard for me to readily appreciate the one I was sitting in tonight. I sat down on the love seat and immediately he started massaging my neck. Here we were in a top class hotel (sure it was top class to me) and this man was still treating me like a lady. Come to think of it, he could have easily grabbed me and thrown me onto the bed, pulled up my dress and roughed me up like I'm nothing! That's happened to me before by other men who treated me like I was just a piece of meat. But not Kev. He was a real gentleman and wasn't trying to take advantage of me in any way. Instead, he treated me royally, like a lady, someone whom he really loved. I wondered if he treated his wife like that. I kind of doubted that. I asked why he was so good to me and he explained that he treated me like that because he loved me and that he didn't even treat his wife that g---, his voice trailed. "Shhh," he interrupted, with his finger covering his lips, signaling me to be quiet. My voice wasn't even all that audible for anyone else to hear. Anyway, I obeyed. I figured he wanted me to be quiet just in case I accidentally uttered a peep. Well, I wasn't so crazy. I knew the script and I played my role very well. He knew darn well, too, that I wouldn't be so stupid to make any utterances that would get him caught or otherwise jeopardize our affair. Furthermore, I'd never do anything stupid to make him not want me.

I knew the code and I respected the code, I played by the rules and that was why he loved me so much. I always knew when his wife was on the phone, I knew when to shut up, to hold my corners and be silent. I pretended not to listen to their conversation but I couldn't help but notice how affectionate he was toward her. Ughhh! I cringed. This was contrary to what he always told me. I wondered what they were laughing about and if this lady knew that he was with me in a fancy room, about to make sweet love to me and get all the things done to him that she didn't do! I wondered if she knew he didn't love her. Well, if she didn't know, I knew. He told me he didn't really want her and that he couldn't wait to leave her. He assured me that he just needed a little more time to sort things out because they had so much together, which was what was making it so difficult for him to leave her. He and I were "creeping" around for six months and it had been the same excuse all that time. Oh, how I wanted him to be lying, typical of what most men do, but deep down I believed he was not.

I felt the magic when he stared into my eyes. I could smell the love pouring from him when he stared at me so sensuously. I was assured of his love because of how he'd hold me so tightly those few hours we'd spend at nights before he had to rush home to his wife. I knew because he said I was better than her in so many ways. He said that I was sexier, I was a better lover, I made him laugh, and that he enjoyed spending every minute with me.

How long was this euphoria going to last? The point is, I didn't care. This moment was ours. It was mine, and I was reveling in it as long as it lasted. I'd rather live in my little fantasy world because it made me complete, than accept the reality of the situation and be in agony. I was aware of the hell he was enduring at home. He and his wife were not seeing eye to eye, he told me and I believed him. He was still talking and I was still listening. It was a long conversation. This woman was cutting into our time and it was making me mad, I just couldn't show that I was mad, though. Not that I respected her position, but she was his wife. She had the upper hand and she came before me. She was in the front and I was on the sideline. Well, for that moment. So, I sat still until the "coach blew the whistle." He ended the conversation by saying, "OK, baby, I love you. See you soon."

He only told her that to make her feel good, I knew that, and I assured myself every time he said that to her. Then, I realized that a wave of jealousy suddenly overcame me and I was breathing heavily. I was upset and was having a hard time controlling my emotions. He tried to explain to me that that was just what he was telling her because that's what she liked to hear and it kept the peace between them. So, I wondered if he was doing the same thing to me. Telling me shit I wanted to hear because he thought I like to hear it and it made me feel good. They say loose lips sink ships so, I was being very guarded with what I said. I just didn't want to make him angry. I fought hard to hold my tongue because I really wanted to interrogate him, but, I didn't want him to tell me that I was acting like her, so I kept quiet.

As he turned toward the bathroom the perfect idea hit. I pulled out my cell phone and positioned it vertically, hidden behind the flower vase on the nightstand. He would never pay attention to that. So, I stripped down, kept my heels on, and, as soon as I heard him flush the toilet, it was on...lights...camera ...action!

I wasn't going to be his fool anymore. It was important that I started to gather all the evidence I could in preparation for the moment when he finally dumped his wife. I was going to make sure she left him so that he could be mine once and for all. I had it all planned out. She was going to be well entertained by some crucial footage. I hit the record button and lead him from the bathroom right into my cell phone view where all the live, top of the hour action was in full force. The recording had begun…. Boy, did I give her a show! I had him screaming, toe curling, panting and shouting my name and calling me "Jesus" like I was his savior. I made sure that during our bumping and grinding I asked him again, "Who's better, baby? Who gives it to you better?" He screamed my name over and over and I knew that once she saw this it would be enough to prove he loved me, and loved me more. Was I betraying him? Well, I don't think so; neither did I feel that I was being deceptive. Truth was, I didn't feel an ounce of guilt. I was simply making life much easier for him as he made his transition from his wretched marriage to a life of contentment, peace and happiness. Something needed to be done and I was going to be the woman to do it! I lay it on him so good that he just stumbled, collapsed in exhaustion and fell asleep right on top of my plump breast like he was drugged. And the recorder was still on. Then, I grabbed my phone and managed to throw in a few selfies so that I could send them along with the video. Perfect combination!

I had her number months ago but I never had the guts to dial it or text it until now. I had done all of my research and had become completely obsessed with her. I scanned her Facebook page everyday, all up on her Instagram, her Pinterest and even her Tumbler. I knew where she worked, her favorite color and even her daily routines.

Be careful of the side woman. She can be very dangerous and evil, especially if you mess with her stuff. I had become exactly that! I knew he would be pissed if I sent the video and pictures, but she needed to know me and feel what I felt whenever I saw her with him.

So, carefully I typed her number into my phone. Attached the video and pictures. My heart was racing and my fingers were shaking. He was sleeping sound like a baby. Then, I contemplated...Should I send it? I knew she would be devastated. But, wasn't that the objective? Or perhaps I didn't want to hurt her but being with him was hurting her enough. My mind was made. She needed to know the truth. My finger jumped. Sent! This was the revelation. I held my phone in my hand...waiting...waiting.

I could see the bubbles moving. She was writing back! Oh, God. I imagined her response. Sadness, anger and confusion. I didn't want her to find out like this, but better now than later. Better now than never!

Ding! My phone beeped. She had responded. I held the phone up nervously to read her response. I was nervous as hell! "Nice video and pics. You look as desperate as he described. I see he took you to the hotel I suggested. He deserves a treat! He said he'd never take me to such a low- class whorehouse as that was reserved for hoodrats like you. I'm better than a three-hour, $57.99-dollar thrill, even if it was strictly for a role-play game. I told him he should take a whore like Sydney, his side chick. I'm

glad he listened. When he wakes up, tell him to shower first, clean

his teeth thoroughly and hurry home to Whitney, his wife."

Dear Sydney,

I know it's hard loving someone who has no intention to commit, is unwilling to share a portion of himself, let alone to give you his all. But why would you give yourself to someone who doesn't claim you as his woman? You may say that you're OK with being the woman on the side, but deep down, no one respects a sidepiece. There's better out there for you, and you deserve more. Why settle for a piece of a man when it's a whole man somewhere who wants to love you genuinely and unconditionally? Put yourself in the woman's shoes and think about your reaction if your man had a side chick. I'm sure you wouldn't appreciate it, and neither would she. No matter how good he makes you feel, you are not a hidden secret. Do not be anyone's waste or convenience; a woman of your caliber must be known to the world, not to be cast aside and rejected.

He has to either decide whether he's going to be with you or her, but it cannot be both and there's absolutely no in between. No secret dates, no hidden, cheap motel rooms, no lonely holidays and missing on important days all because he's with his main woman. Be better than he expects you to be, put your cap a little distance away where it's hard for anyone to reach. Set your expectations higher than you can even imagine reaching them; they are attainable! Take your heart out of his lap and put it in your feet and walk away.

I guarantee you, you'll gradually acquire true happiness with every step you take. One day at a time.

Sincerely,

Juliet C.

Lying Latoya

I quickly got in touch with my connect to see how much a fake ID would cost. Dammit man! These were the moments I regretted being young and secretly wished that I didn't have to wait all of seven whole months before I was considered "legal." Clubb Skyy was having the most outrageous party Saturday night for the city's most popular tattoo artist, Mr. Rick Inks, the man himself. And your girl just had to be in her spot that night. I wouldn't miss that party for a million bucks! Now, due to popular demand, instead of the usual $300, the ID price had gone up to $500. Five hundred damn dollars! I owed this money to my mom but I could just tell her I was robbed or something because, come hell or high water, I had to find it. This was one time I couldn't complain about 500 dollars because this was my gateway to meet the man of my dreams. I must pay it if I'm going to meet my future husband. I told the ID guy to put me down as Latoya Walker and my age as 26. I also enclosed my photograph sporting a sassy ice- blonde hair style. My mom always told me that my blonde wig made me look twice my age, so I figured that that would add some credibility to my ID story. Now, I wouldn't blame you for asking why would any young woman want to look twice her age. It's simple. Looking older was going to get me Rick. And if you knew who the great Rick was, then you'd not hasten to judge me. I wasn't going to pass up on this single, fine ass Caribbean god. He was royal, as royal as the Caribbean Sea. He would not pass me...nope, not for anything! I had heard about him from around the way. I saw him on many pics, but he was a hard man to find anywhere, not even on social media. So, as you see, for me, this was a golden opportunity to meet him. Call me desperate, but this was it, tonight was going to be the night I'd do anything.

I walked straight along the path leading to Club Skyy, rocking my sexy ass and flashing my 26-inch, blonde, lace-front wig. My dress was tighter than a latex, and I stuffed my size 26 bosom to a flattering 38, just to add a little more plumpness to my breasts. The Kardashians had nothing on me! My lashes were as long as my sparkling nails and I could hardly see, but the little vision that I had was taking me straight to my destination, and that was all that mattered. The doorman was very serious about his ID checks and the more he looked and scanned each woman's identification, the more nervous and uneasy I began to feel about carrying a fake ID.

The queue was moving quickly along for the bag and ID check. I was next to be searched. Just then I saw the black Escalade pull up. It was him! My Caribbean king! Damnnn. He looked even better in person. I wanted to fake a heart attack right there in the damn line or dash closer to him and faint, hoping to get some CPR, but I held my composure and my lies for when I needed them most. His grand entrance and fancy entourage had created enough crowd distraction so much that the doorman was hardly paying us any attention. He barely looked at my ID as he was trying to beg for a selfie with one of the sidekicks. He just made a fleeting glance and a sloppy search and motioned me to keep it moving. I was so relieved.

I could see that Rick had already made his way upstairs to the VIP in the club. Six men dressed in black stood at the bottom of the stairs and the only people who were fortunate to get past them were those sexy little bottle servers in skinny black dresses, bunny ears and bottles. Shit, I was wearing a sexy black dress but where was I going to find bunny ears and a bottle from? I eyed them closely and waited for the perfect opportunity. Luck was obviously on my side because I was just in time to see one waitress take a quick stop in the restroom. I crawled unnoticed and inched a littler closer to the entrance and got on her case. I watched her with those cute little bunny ears, but soon they would be mine. She headed inside the stall and, to my dismay, she did not take them off her head. Ughhh! How was I going to get them? I couldn't just snatch them off her head like that, that would be trouble, to be caught stealing a waitress' bunny ears from the bathroom. Just imagine if my Prince Charming Rick saw the commotion of a girl being carried out by security because she stole a pair of damn bunny ears. No way. I had to think fast.... I was good at this.

She emerged from the stall and immediately I noticed a little lady sitting by the bathroom mirror selling combs, brushes, gum, candy, water...shit, you name it, she had it all laid out there on the counter. I couldn't believe it, but I didn't have time to question her personal retail store she had set up in the restroom. I glanced at the waitress and quickly sparked up a conversation, "There's something in the back of your hair, not sure if it's gum or what, but it looks kinda gooey. I can try and get it out for you if you want." The waitress was very grateful that I was trying to help her, so I motioned for the little old lady selling her goods to pass me a comb. She looked at me questioningly as if to say, "Bitch, stop lying, what gum do you see? I don't see no gum." Before she opened her toothless mouth, I slid her a 20-dollar bill and she quickly passed me the comb. I carefully removed those precious bunny ears off the waitress' head and held them in my hands while pretending to remove the gum from her hair. Then, I suckered her into a conversation and, within seconds she forgot I had her bunny ears in my hand. "I need you to take this order right now, baby," a young man appeared at the door and informed her. She rushed out of the stall leaving me holding onto my priceless bunny ears. They were mine. Whew! That was close. Now, all I needed were a bottle and a tray and I'd blend right in. I was on a mission.

I avoided the waitress whose ears I had stolen. I didn't want her to see me and figure out that I had manipulated her. I was scared of any form of backlash, too; next thing the whole club would be hearing about stolen bunny ears and humiliate me like a dog. I'd rather die! Standing by another bar I spotted a few women grabbing bottles and trays that had sparkling lights on them. This was my first time in an actual club and I was amazed at everything I saw. My cute bunny ears were carefully perched on my head as I skipped around, trying to mingle with the other cuties. One of the girls grabbed my wrist and pulled me closer to the bar and whispered, "Hey, grab a tray, we have a big order up there and we need your help." Yes! Was this the opportunity I had been waiting for? I think I finally had a reason to get up to where Rick was and deliver a bottle. I grabbed a tray and followed the line of waitresses and marched upstairs. I concentrated hard to avoid a fall, to look cute, to seek and get attention, while at the same time balancing a bottle of sparkling fireworks. After tonight, I had a new respect for all waitresses, too. It might look simple on the outside but their work involves a lot of hard work and scheming. You may not need a degree, but you have to get with the program. And, damn, there he was...sitting handsomely and elegantly as ever, covered in a million tattoos. My baby! I placed the bottle on one of the tables near him and flashed a smile I had been rehearsing for days. I leaned in. "Hi...Hi...." The music was so loud I don't know if he could hear me or if he was ignoring me. I felt embarrassed. I tried again. Screaming over the music, I yelled, "Heyyy, I love your tattoos. They're cute just like the wearer. I'm a tattoo artist myself. Just opened up my own shop."

I guess I must have caught his attention with the word "tattoo" because he stood up and pulled me closer to a quieter area. "Cool, where did you get licensed?" I pretended not to hear him over the DJ but the truth was I didn't have a clue about tattoos. I was just looking for a reason to talk to him. I didn't mean to lie... but it worked. See, I had saved up all my lies for the perfect moment. Then he leaned in again, "So, you do tattoos and a side job as a waitress? Pretty cool I guess. You're the first tattoo artist I've ever met without a single tattoo, though," he continued, looking suspicious. I thought for a short second and then lied again. "I have them underneath, in areas you can't see," I chimed in with a mischievous smile. He eyed me from head to toe and then replied, "Oh, OK, I see now...well, who knows, maybe one day I'll get to see them," he said loudly.

We talked for about 30 minutes, and during the conversation I had given him all lies about myself. I had lied so much my tongue was feeling heavy. He didn't know my real name, real age, real occupation, real nothing. I wondered what he'd think if he found out that I was a struggling 20-year-old college student who lived at home with her mom. The thought crossed my mind but I would make sure that he would never find out. We exchanged numbers and I left feeling confident that I had him right where I wanted him. I had gotten my man.

Weeks went by and Rick and I had been kicking it really hard. I was struggling to keep up with all the stories and lies I had told him...like that my house was flooded, so I was living with my mom, and that my tattoo shop was being remodeled that's why I wasn't working there at the time we met. I told him I quit working at the night club to spend more time getting my shop ready, and didn't say that my real name wasn't Latoya or that I wasn't really 26. The stories were so many that I myself could hardly keep track. I desperately wanted this man to like me and want me; I thought the only way to achieve that was to fabricate stories to get him.

We had developed a closeness with each other, and the time had come for Rick and me to get it down. I had been holding off from the night I met him because I didn't know how I was going to explain that I didn't really have one freakin' tattoo all this time. What the hell was he going to think? They had disappeared? The first night I met him I told him that I was plastered with tattoos in hidden places; I'm sure he'll be on the lookout for them. I was a nervous wreck. We met at his house because I wouldn't dare bring a man, worse a grown man, to my mom's house, yet alone to have sex with him.

The mood was set immediately. We had barely reached inside the house when he began kissing me passionately. My breasts were noticeably smaller but he didn't care. He kept right on sucking and caressing them anyway. He didn't know that I was a virgin because I told him otherwise, so I was scared he might have noticed something during the act. I did everything to stall him, but nothing was working. He kept right on until he finally unbuttoned my shirt, unzipped and pulled down my shorts along with my panties. Then the lights flicked on followed by the situation I dreaded. "Baby, where is your hidden ink?" I was tongue-tied. This was one time in my life when I didn't know what lie to flash or what to say. But I thought quickly. "Baby, I know this sounds crazy but I have to admit, all these years I have been doing tattoos, I'm actually afraid of the needle. I'm more scared of the needle more than how I'm afraid of an alligator or say, a snake, believe me." He smiled and told me all I had to do was keep it real with him and that I could have told him all along. I was relieved.

He was right. All I had to do was to keep it real about who I was from the beginning instead of trying so hard to impress. Things don't work out like that all the time. It's like forcing someone to like you under duress. I had lied about everything. And the bottom line was, he didn't know me, he didn't know who I was. He only knew the person I told him I was, the person I lied about all these weeks. Now here we were...having sex and it felt like he was killing me. He was gyrating and pumping me so hard, I was in pain. Was it payback for my sins? I hid the tears and wanted to scream, "STOP!" but I couldn't, and he didn't know it wasn't his fault. I shouldn't have lied.This was not how my first time should have been. I should have been straight up instead of all these falsehoods. I felt even worse when he pulled out, leaving a terrible mess on the sheets. It was blood. My blood... It was my first time.

Rick looked at me in disgust but he didn't bother to ask. It seemed he had caught on to what was happening. He had just popped my cherry! I was in pain as he lay there holding me...silent. Neither one of us said a word but I wondered what he was thinking. Maybe he didn't know that I had been lying about so many things. Maybe all this time he was actually buying it all when I had a chance to come forward with the truth. I didn't know. I huddled there, waiting for him to say something, then, he did. "Toya, let me do you a tattoo. You say you're scared, but let me do you one. Don't be scared, baby, I'll go easy."

I almost didn't answer him. I wanted to tell him so badly that my name wasn't Latoya, it was Charlene. But, I didn't...I couldn't. And truth is, I was really scared of needles. Nevertheless, I got up and let him get to work just to avoid telling anymore lies.

He got to work; he removed all his equipment and laid them on the table. He said he had a really special design he wanted to put on my back. He seemed excited. I almost asked him not to make it visible because I didn't want my mom to see her 20-year-old daughter with a tattoo. How could I tell him that I wasn't 26? So, I had to roll with the punches. Well, I was very happy that he decided to put it on my lower back because it was a little hidden.

I lay prostrate on the chair with my back to him and my ass crack hanging out. This process was more painful than his eight-inch dick I had just felt. It felt like someone was stabbing a knife in my back. After an hour I was wondering what he was designing on me. The intense pain stopped after a while, and I waited anxiously for the drilling to stop as well. Then, he looked at me and said, "I'm done. You can go see." I got up, aching and sore, with a I limp. I wasn't quite sure whether it was the pain from losing my virginity or from a damn ink needle on my back for an hour, but something had me aching all over. I hobbled over to the long wall mirror, eager to see Rick's handiwork. I was anticipating a pleasant surprise, to see what he seemed so excited about. And there it was, in bold, black letters emblazoned across my back. "LYING LATOYA." My heart sank and my mouth dropped to the floor! Rick had given me his permanent stamp.

Dear LaToya,

You can see from this character that lying can lead to harsh unwanted consequences.

We all think we can get away with what we call little white lies. The problem is that those little lies can snowball into great big ones, and then it gets to the point where we don't remember what we said before, and then it gets to the point that our pretend life gets out of control.

So it's best to remember two Golden Rules. The old saying about the tangled web we weave when we start to deceive makes a lot of sense. Your initial lie can get wound up with more subsequent lies to the point that you no longer know what you've already said. And when faced with the truth it then becomes a problem trying to justify what we've already said.

The wisest rule is the one that reminds us that if you always tell the truth you'll never have to remember anything.

So, to avoid entanglements in your life, keep in simple and always keep it true. That way you'll avoid having those never-ending lies leading to consequences you won't like.

Sincerely,

Juliet C.

Cheating Candace

I cautiously aimed the absorbent tip in a downward position then, after peeing on the stick for five seconds, I placed it face up on the counter, just as directed. Two minutes felt like a million years. My breathing was labored, coming in short, heavy spasms, and they felt much longer than usual. Before I read the results, my mind raced back eight weeks prior to the moment that brought me to this home pregnancy test. I just stared with my mouth wide opened.

It was a Monday night; as a matter of fact it was a Friday night. My girls and I were just in time to catch Happy Hour at "Bar Krazy" on Spark Boulevard, to get in on that 2-for-1 drink special. I ordered my usual "Take-'em-Home Daiquiri" with a splash of pineapple and a cherry on top. There was something about that drink that always had me feeling really mellow, free and ready for "the night's catch." Hubby was away on his monthly business trip for the entire weekend and there was no better way to celebrate having the weekend all to myself. Like they say, when the cat's away, the mice will play. And as it is written, so it will be! Playtime was about to begin and I was in search of a big cat. Bar Krazy was super packed tonight, you'd think they were giving away free drinks or free food. I guess everyone was trying to get that special tonight.

We hit the dance floor immediately and from across the room I sniffed out a hunky big cat just staring at me. He was a tall muscular eye candy, eyeing me from head to toe. I eased myself away from the ladies to get a closer view and to clear the area so that they wouldn't be all up in my business. I wasted no time in sliding my wedding ring off; it fell during the process and I hoped that no one realized what I was up to. I quickly tucked it into my back pocket and inched my way closer and closer to the bar near to where his hot ass was standing. The closer I got to him the more I could see that he was sexy as hell for real and that my eyes were not fooling me. He reminded me of Daniel...no, Terrance...wait.... He actually looked like Neil and from the side view, he could even go for that guy Anderson. I think that that was his name. Oh well....

Anyway, I know I'm a married woman, so I wouldn't dare do anything crazy, just making sure that I still had it going on as I tested out my sexiness. Standing at the bar, I placed my horny self right in front of his chest and started grinding my ass against his six pack. His hard steel frame let me know that he was enjoying my moves. Beads of moist sweat dripped on me as he held my waist firmly, forcing my body to throw it back on him. As he began caressing both my ass cheeks, I felt his penis rise like the Chicago Tower Bridge, a sure sign that big cat was ready for a cute little mouse. And, needless to say, this little mousey was ready!

I was anxious to see what he was working with and what was packed away in those tight pants, but with so many startled and jealous eyes glued on us, I couldn't be too brazen, plus my girls would be looking for me any minute. It was time to vanish into an area where I couldn't be seen. Thing was, they knew my routine, so I had to find a more private location to avoid any assumptions or accusations. I grabbed his wrist, headed toward the bathroom and quickly disappeared behind the stall. I became a little worried that he didn't have a condom. Of course, I didn't expect him to be wearing one, but every man should at least have one in the event that the "mice are on the loose." I usually carry one in my wallet but I was slipping tonight. We squeezed our bodies into the tight space against the door of the stall and began kissing and caressing. Yes, the liquor was definitely working because I never usually kiss them on the first night. Well, I never kiss them at all because it's never usually a second, third or any other night after the first one anyway. It was all about "get what I can get, and then call it quits" kind of thing. Nothing serious. That's my mantra...that's what I lived by! The rank smell of the partially flushed toilet was nauseating, but my body was steaming and I wanted him so desperately that I was willing to endure the fleeting discomfort. I unbuckled my jeans while he pulled his long penis out. It was rock hard and I anticipated every inch to be thrust deep inside my snatch. I bent over while spreading my legs like a little puppy taking a leak.

"I'm married," he whispered. "Me, too, now stick it in harder already!" I yelled impatiently. Instantly we were fucking like two teenagers on prom night. My moments of excitement usually lasted for five to six minutes and I needed to be fully intoxicated for any minutes past ten. It never took long afterward to snap back to reality, then, I remember I am a married woman, in a committed relationship. I would try to remind myself but I took a break and realized that I was just having a good time, enjoying someone else besides my husband. Simple as that.

Then, just as how it began, it ended. Just like that. I pulled up my denims, buttoned my shirt and walked out of the bathroom as if I was just powdering my make-up. Nothing had happened. I was a pro at this and nobody would ever be able to tell that I was just locked down fucking in a tight, dimly lit, foul 30-inch stall. The plan was to always appear calm, cool and collected where nobody could tell what I was up to. I had it down pat, and that's how I always got away with it. I was the Queen of Cheating!

Admittedly, several thoughts crossed my mind as I headed back to my friends. What if someone had seen us enter the bathroom? What if my husband found out about this one? What if he had something like a disease? What if...but, most importantly...what the hell was his name? The name didn't really matter that much anyway, but damn, I could have at least asked him.

I tried my best to stay emotionally detached whenever I cheated with someone because I didn't want my feelings getting the best of me. I looked at it just as how a man did his cheating and tried to pattern off that. It was just sex...no emotions, no falling in love...nothing more, and in the morning, I could wake up and carry on with my day like it never happened.

I know that that sounds strange coming from a woman, but I had been cheated on enough to the point where I just didn't care anymore about hurting someone's feelings. Especially a lying, cheating ass man! My feelings had been shredded my entire life. I had never been with a man who didn't cheat; in fact, I don't even know a man who didn't cheat. I think my dad was the pioneer for cheating because he had a different woman every day of the week. I saw my mom allow him to have multiple women, but that wasn't going to be the story of my marriage. Having a no-good, nasty, two-timing man...oh, no! My theory was that all men cheated no matter how good we were to them. So, I vowed that the next relationship I'm ever in I was going to do the same thing. Well, it's just a mere coincidence that my dear husband was the recipient. I knew it was wrong. I had no morals or values that guided my thought process; I didn't see anything that was so immoral about someone sneaking in a little fun on the side. It was exciting, thrilling...and I finally understood why a man did it. I couldn't stop.

I met up with my friends back at the same spot where I had left them. I touched up a bit with perfume and munched on a stick of gum. Not a hair was out of place but a slightly bent acrylic that I immediately straightened out. And the barrage of questions began, "Girl, where were you?" I immediately changed the subject, avoided the conversation and was ready to end the night back in the comforts of my home where I could be who I wanted to be without having to be pretentious and explaining away myself. Plus I needed a shower after having five minutes of rough, aggressive sex in a stink box! There was sticky cum crystallizing between my thighs and I was starting to feel a bit itchy. Nothing but a solid bar of Zest or Caress could take away this uncomfortable feeling.

I called my husband as soon as I got home and told him how much fun I had at Happy Hour with my girls. He sounded a bit suspicious but I continued to act as if no "rule" was broken. I usually called him to check in so he at least thinks I'm at home being his faithful fairy. He was happy that I had made my usual check-in, because, like he always said, he doesn't want to have any man out there lusting or even dancing with his queen. I just giggled innocently and assured my baby that all was well.

Then, the night was drifting and I was feeling lonely. The 2-for-1s were wearing off and the only itch that needed to be scratched this time was my uncontrollable hormones. They were screaming for another dick to put this body to sleep. Yes, I was a savage. Some even described me as a nasty, gutter bitch that was OK with having five dicks in one night, but nobody's opinion mattered and I didn't care what anyone thought. I only cared about how my body felt, and I was waiting to feel even better tonight. I was clean, new sheets were laid, and all I needed was some company. Who was going to fill this empty space next to me tonight? I flipped to my call log and scrolled: Sam, Robert, Damien, Orlando, Carlos...hmmm...none replied to my texts. I guess they were tired of me using them or maybe they didn't remember who I was. Who could I call? Well, tonight someone was going to remember! Greg. That's who! His broke ass would be here in no time. And I was right, 20 minutes after my call, he was ringing the door bell. As soon as he walked in he dropped his boxers and we hit it. I hated having sex in the same bed I shared with Craig, but Greg was family, so I made an exception for him. Greg hated to see the pics of me and Craig around the house. I guess the guilt might have set in on him but it wasn't setting in on me. I actually liked to see his pictures on the nightstand while I lay next to another man. I would look straight in his face, not even a wink, while I was having sex with someone else and pretend he was watching me. It made me feel good to know that I was able to do whatever I desired without caring about how it affected anyone else. Kind of the same way men did me throughout my relationships. Only this time I was in control.

It was a fun night with Greg but there was no way he was going to be able to stay overnight. Besides, Craig would be back home tomorrow and I had to wash my sheets and throw away any condoms or evidence that might have been left in the house. I dumped three condoms from the garbage but I realized I was missing one. I wondered who didn't strap up this weekend. Well, I didn't have the time to figure it out tonight because I had to get the house fresh. I couldn't have my husband lying in the same bed where I just gave it up to another man. Or should I? Nah. I decided I wasn't going to do him so dirty so I sorted the linens and washed them.

The weeks went by slowly, then my husband, Craig, caught a break from his usual weekend business trips. During that time, he managed to stay home and we had a lot of time to make up for all the sex we were missing. Well, he was missing! I couldn't believe that I didn't desire to be with another man and was quite content with having one dick for these few weeks. Perhaps my husband was satisfying me enough, or was he? It was the first time I was ignoring text messages and SMS pics of dicks asking, "Do you want me tonight?" At first, I thought I was finally becoming this faithful wife. Like something erupted in my spirit and washed all my sins away. I was hopeful that I was a changed woman. I wanted to change but couldn't find the will power to do so. Somehow I was baffled as to why I didn't have the urge to mess around with not a single piece of penis. It couldn't be. I was aware that something was wrong and that I was acting differently.

My sex drive had depleted and I didn't feel horny, I wasn't thinking as much about sex. This was a sure sign that something wasn't right.

Then, I glanced at the calendar and rushed to check the dates. I was off completely and never even noticed. My "Aunt Mary" didn't visit me this month? I became nervous and started counting again. Was I really eight days late on my period? Again, I counted. Dear God…I was panicking. I took some deep breaths and slumped on the bed, the thought of being pregnant terrified me. What if I were pregnant? But wait. Don't panic, I comforted myself. Craig has been home and I haven't slept with anyone else of late. So, this is some basic math. If I'm pregnant, it has to be my husband's.

I shared the good news of the possibility of being pregnant with my husband. "Pregnant?" he replied, a bit surprised and confused. "Are you sure, Candace? How do you know?" I explained to him that I wasn't sure but all the bits and pieces were adding up and it seemed as if I was right. He stared blankly, wringing his palms for a few minutes. No utterances, only sighs. I don't know if he was happy or in shock or what. I asked him to get me an EPT but he didn't respond. He then left and came back 20 minutes later with a test.

So, here it goes... time for the home pregnancy results. My two minutes had expired long ago. "Craig, what does it say, baby. What does it say?" There was a long pause and then he walked out with the test in his hand, shaking. "Says you're pregnant," he responded, shaking his head.

Craig insisted that I take another one, so I took three more and the results were the same. Positive. I made an appointment right away to confirm if this were true because Craig was in disbelief. Not me, though, I was OK with it and I wasn't the least bit worried. Perhaps this was the catalyst I needed to put a trap to my heels. This might just slow me down.

The sun had barely risen the following day and we were on our way to the appointment. I sat on the table, trying to appear composed while assuring Craig that everything would be OK. Craig sat about six feet across from me still looking confused and worried about the result. Dr. Lacoste walked in, and with her usual formidable style, she held out her hand and, with her broad, radiant smile, she said, "Congratulations! You are definitely pregnant! You must be a very happy couple today." Craig was stone cold. I thanked her and smiled at Craig. He didn't return the smile. Instead, he stared at the doctor, uttered a slight moan and asked, "Doc, I know it's kinda early, and my request might sound a bit premature, but tell me, is there any way we can determine the paternity of the baby round about now?"

Wow! What on earth was he doing? Was he serious? I was angry and humiliated. Right in the doctor's presence this man was embarrassing me. I hung my head, crestfallen. He had destroyed this moment and shattered my pride. But I wanted her to be able to go through with the process, to take as much blood as she can to prove to this asshole that this was his baby! He was going to be the one embarrassed as shit. Not me. This situation even made me more confident that he was the cheater. Why the fuck was he questioning me and making covert accusations? Maybe he was the one hiding something. Well, we shall see.

"I'm sorry, but we can't tell paternity this early, sir; however, if we take your blood and the baby's blood we can definitely see whether they match." We both agreed and allowed them to draw blood from all three of us, the fetus, Craig and me. We had to wait an hour before the results came back. It was torture. We sat in an uncomfortable silence that seemed like an eternity. The room was cold and we shivered as we waited. No one spoke. The stillness was unbearable coupled with the suspension. There we sat, in the cold room, waiting. Then, finally, the nurse appeared. My heart skipped a beat as Craig showed no emotion. "Yep, it's a match."

"How could this be possible?" Craig questioned adamantly. Was he really trying to claim that the blood result could be misleading? "Like damn, Craig, it's yours!" I yelled. At this point I didn't care who was listening. I was tired of him insulting me, disputing the test result and denying our unborn fetus after his blood type was a match. Dr Lacoste seemed curious and baffled at his questionable actions. "What's going on here, Craig? What's the problem?" she asked.

He answered nervously, "Doc, it's nothing, I...I'm sorry, but it's just that I had a vasectomy and I didn't think it was possible to make a baby. The doctor assured me that there's no way I could get any woman pregnant!" he blurted. I didn't have the desire to have kids with you. A few months ago, while on a business trip, I had a vasectomy. I wanted to tell you ---I did, ... but I knew you'd be hurt. I'm very sorry but there's no way you could be pregnant with my baby. Can she be doc? Craig held his head down in disbelief and curiously waited for a response from the doctor. I laughed hysterically, then, Dr. Lacoste looked at Craig and said, "Well, you are one of the rare cases where a baby was conceived and born after a vasectomy procedure."

Craig looked over at me, touched my hand gently and smiled at me. I knew it was his way of apologizing and he was embarrassed that he was accusing me of cheating. I sighed in relief and quickly returned his smile. I then reached across, hugged him tightly and kissed him on the cheeks. He blushed like a child and I gave him a playful bite. For once he seemed happy. Little did his dumb ass know! I was just lucky that the fetus was his and that I wasn't caught after all. So much for being smart! Dr. Lacoste headed toward the door, but before she finally exited, she turned around as she continued laughing.

"Craig, I really hope you feel better. I just want to assure you that you are the father because the match is 99.9 percent positive and the only other possible match would be if you had a twin brother, which is unlikely," she reassured him, and continued giggling all the way to the door and along the hallways.   "Well, actually, I am a twin."

Dr. Lacoste's face grew serious. "Oh, I didn't know you were a twin, Craig. What's his name?"   "Ask Cheating Candace," he fired back.   Dammit, shit! I was caught. Just like that. This evil had finally caught up with me.

Craig knew I was cheating with his brother all along! "Greg. His twin brother's name is Greg," I interrupted.

Dear Candace,

Men cheat. Men hurt women. Men break women's hearts. Men destroy hopes, lives and dreams then go on like it's nobody business, like nothing happened and still claim they love you. Their one night stands are exactly just that, and come the next day, they don't even think about it, they won't even remember your name.

On the contrary, women are different. We are the bedrock of the family, truly emotional creatures who love hard and deep and we can't easily sleep around without gaining some type of feelings no matter how much we try, we just can't. Webster describes the woman as the female who is capable of giving birth, nourishment, virtue and love. We are creatures like no other, we just cannot be compared. We can't do what a man does, and even if we do, we can't get away with it so, don't even try. So much for society's double standards.

Well, let me make one thing straight here, truth is sometimes stranger than fiction, don't think that every man cheats. There are some really great men out there who value their relationships and their women. So, if you are trying to be like a man... be like the faithful few who put their love before their feelings, those who treat their women with respect and, of course, there are the blessed few who make responsible decisions.

Sincerely,

Juliet C.

Nagging Nikki

Nagging Nikki: Seven calls. Six voicemails. Twelve text messages. I'm about to go off on him...then, finally, he answers. About time! I don't care if he's out with his mom for her birthday, he's got to make more quality time for me and I'm starving. After all, I am his wife and we should be spending all, if not, most of our time together. I know he's heard the phrase leave to cleave. He's too much of a mama's boy and I'm tired of how much time he wants to spend with her.

As soon as he answered, I started with my detailed food order. "Uhm, get me rice, chicken, salad, extra cucumbers, dressing...wait, no...no cucumbers, hold the beans, aaagh...no sauce on the meat, extra sauce for the salad and a diet soda with a little bit of ice, make sure the cup is full. I'm warning you, just a little ice!" I spoke so loudly you'd think a microphone was stuck up my ass. "Oh, and, please, make sure you check the doggone bag."

After I was done with the specifics, I sent him a follow-up text just to make sure he got it right. You see, Jaxson is really idiotic and requires constant reminders like a kid. I'm not bashing him but I'm sure he was going to get something wrong. He slammed down the phone before saying his usual, "Yeah, whatever." It's OK. He can slam it down all he wants. I'll check his ass when he comes home.

Sometimes he can be a great husband and father but I only wished he pulled his weight a lot more around the house. I'm just so sick of him leaving the toilet seat up, his toothbrush in the kitchen sink and his clothes all over the damn floor. I decided to help him get a little more organized by leaving him a daily "honey to-do list." The honey to-do list had manageable reminders for simple things I needed him to get done throughout the day...like, don't forget to take out the garbage, help the boys with homework, sing the ABCs with the baby, stop by the grocery store, remove the clothes from the dryer and have the meat seasoned by the time I got home so that we can cook dinner together. Yep... Together! He was crazy if he thought he was going to be lying around on the couch watching TV while I was sweating over a hot stove, cooking dinner for him. I know he works hard on his job and is probably exhausted himself but relationships are about teamwork. Besides, had he submitted the resumés I completed last month for him, he'd probably have a better job in an office and would be making way more money. Then, he'd be able to afford the mini van I want him to get instead of driving that raggedy old car he continues to embarrass me with.

Actually, had he continued working with my father at the car shop like I told him to, he'd be part owner now, but nooo, he insisted on following his damn "dreams" working in construction instead of doing what I wanted him to do. Listen, it's not that I want to annoy him and rule his life, but he's got to take my lead and listen to me. I wouldn't tell him anything wrong because I always know what I'm talking about, and so far, I've been pretty much right about everything. I'm just tired of him because he's extremely disorganized and irresponsible. This man doesn't even know how to manage his money, so I can't really trust him to make "grown-up" decisions. It's so bad that I had to make sure his direct deposit goes straight into my account and from there I give him money for gas and other necessities, and I watch those stupid "necessities," too. Things he claims he must have. Too many times I tried to give him his own debit card but he couldn't handle it. Daily transactions and spending money on foolish things like fast food and lotto tickets that his slight ass stands no chance of winning anyway. The only luck he ever had was when he married me. Which I still can't understand how I married a man with love handles?

I have him on a pretty strict diet to get rid of them though...no soda, no sweets, no snacks and pretty much no fatty foods that will contribute to him being out of shape. But no matter the diet, he continues to eat badly. Often I find receipts in his car that lets me know he's ordering lots of double cheeseburgers, milk shakes and large fries! Yuck. I don't allow him to have any cheat days, so I guess he tries to get away with it when he's at work...which is why I signed him up for the gym and he refuses to take advantage of his membership. I keep telling him he's got to shed the fat because I want him to lose 10 pounds before my job has our annual Christmas party. I don't want my co-workers thinking he's a good-for-nothing fat ass. Now, I go as far as making sure he's wearing his fit bit, waist trainer, taking his muscle boosters every day and that he counts his daily calorie intake. Seven hundred calories per day is usually my limit for him. Every morning I have him drink a green shake instead of his favorite

"two bowls of sugary Pebbles cereal."

I hate to hear him smack and slurp milk from a spoon anyway, and licking the spilled milk off his fingers, so I'm constantly reminding him to chew with his mouth closed and ensure that he bites his food at least 32 times before swallowing. He tends to be a glutton, and I'm always warning him that we are eating to live...not vice versa.

People may think that I'm micro-managing this grown ass man but, understand this, he is my man, and both of us benefit when he is in good shape, therefore, my goal is for him to be healthy and fit, which explains why I set his alarm clock for 4 a.m. so that before work he can get up and do his two-mile jog. This will help him from waddling like a damn penguin and get rid of that fat jiggly ass and unattractive beer belly. He isn't allowed to drink alcohol unless it's a holiday so I don't know how a beer belly got there to begin with. It's so difficult maneuvering around a shaky belly during sex. We are working on a more attractive body but I can only fix one thing with him at a time and my list is pretty long, so I've got to start at the top. I hate having to speak to him like he's one of our children but he's got to know how I feel and he has to stop making me feel as if my concerns about him aren't valid. After all, I am his wife and my opinion about him should count even more so than his own.

So, our big argument started yesterday and this how it all went down. I came home from a long hard day at work only to find Jaxson knocked out on my pristine, white leather sofa. First off, he broke my very serious rule. Number 1, this man knows I don't allow anyone to step foot in my living room, let alone to be sleeping and, worse, during the daytime. Number 2, it's a school night, and the kids were watching TV, and not one thing on his to-do list was crossed off! Talk about being pissed! I immediately woke his lazy ass up. I work the same eight hours he does, so I'm just as tired as he is, yet I don't have time to watch TV and take naps, especially with an 8, 4 and 1-year-old. If I'm going to have another baby in a year like I planned, he's got to start getting his shit together because with another child comes more responsibilities and I will not be doing it alone. What gives him the right to think that he can just lie here and sleep his ass off when he has things to do?

I asked the kids to stay in their room before I interrupted his precious sleep on my white sofa. I didn't want them to hear what I was about to say to their father and I'm sure they were tired of hearing me having to tell him how to be a man almost everyday. Even though the boys are young, and our youngest can barely talk, Jaxson still has to set good examples for them and know that they are watching his every move. To me, he wasn't even being a good role model...well, at least not the way I was teaching him to be one. Shoving his shoulder aggressively, I yelled "Jaxson, Jaxson, wake up!" He was lucky I didn't blow my bull horn and terrorize his ass like I usually do when he snores too loud at night. He woke up with his usual annoyed face. He annoyed? The nerves he had...I should be the one pissed. Before he could even answer me or ask why I was screaming, I began my all-too-familiar rant. I didn't want to hear a word he was about to say. I went on and on to him for about an hour about how nothing was done that I left for him do. I'm sick and tired of him telling me how lucky I am and how he works so hard to be a great provider for his family. Was he kidding me? He's doing everything he's supposed to be doing so he wasn't getting any accolades or rewards from me. What did he expect? A pat on the shoulder and some chocolate candies? I was raised knowing that the man is supposed to be the bread winner, the provider, the protector and the head of his family, so, if he was waiting for an applause from me, he had better sit his ass still because he'd be waiting until Judgment Day. For the most part he shouldn't have any complaints. I allowed him to do everything except to be the head and that was solely because he didn't want to do anything MY way and it was either MY way or no way at all!

To be honest, I don't even think I'm that difficult to be married to. I think most men would be happy to have a woman to help keep them organized, give them advice, set their schedules, tell them what to wear, help them eat healthy and teach them how to be a man. I was making life easier for him. But not Jaxson. He obviously didn't appreciate all that I was doing for him. He would get annoyed with any of my requests, no matter how simple. He said I was too aggravating and that I complained too damn much, but I believe he was just an impatient person who couldn't deal with all the affection, the attention and take directions well. What was so hard about changing the bathroom lights when I asked, or painting the kitchen walls once a year, or driving slower over the speed bumps, listening to Gospel music during our car rides or taking me to the grocery store once a week? It was the little things that would make him become agitated with me. I'd look around at my friends and their relationships and then I'd think about how much their man does for them compared to what Jaxson does for me. Every night I give him the run down about everything my friends have and what their man is doing for them. I simply want him to know that those are the things I would like him to do for me. I prayed to God that it'll finally sink in one day and he will make an effort to try and change. I gave him a list of successful men that he should aspire to be. He argues that I'm never satisfied. Well, I disagree. Is it too much to ask him to rub my feet when I get off work after walking around in those cheap high heels he bought me, or for him to go to church on Sundays instead of watching the game? Is it too much for him to eat dinner at my mom's with my family or sit with me throughout my manicure, or to engage him in listening to my stories about work? I don't think I'm asking for a lot. After five years of marriage, I don't understand why he's not become accustomed to our routine. Other than his to-do list he has a big calendar where I mark down everything I have planned for our month. Out of 28-30 days in a month, I'm only asking for 20. Damn, I should demand more. What does he really have to do other than spend time with me? The other days I expect him to spend with the kids and he even has a problem with that. Then he has the guts to ask me, "So, when do I have time for me, Jaxson? I need my me-time, you know?"

"Me? Listen, which me Jaxson you talking 'bout?" I said in my stern tone. "When you get married, you give up the me for us. Seems you have a problem separating me from us?" You must understand that it's no more thinking about yourself. This is a relationship that requires full-time commitment in all aspects and obviously he wasn't ready to do that. My friends and family think I'm ungrateful because I complain so much. They feel that I should be happy to have an upright, humble, obedient man who takes care of his family financially, emotionally and spiritually. But I disagree. They don't see everything I see...and I'm very realistic. He's simply not meeting up to my standards, and when compared to my friends' relationships, I think he can be a much better spouse.

Point is...I need a break from him until he realizes my worth. I am the only one who knows what's best for his life and until he gets that, I am done.

So after 10 more minutes of him listening to my complaints, I told him to get the hell out of my house. I don't care that he pays most of the bills. It's still my house and I wanted him out. Reluctantly, he packed up his things and left. Deep down I think he wasn't reluctant at all though but actually happy to have a break from his routine. Soon he's going to wake up and smell the roses and then call me begging to come home. He will realize that he is throwing away his life, and that I'm the best thing that ever happened to him.

Two days later: Welp! I guess I was wrong about him smelling the roses after all. It's been two days since Jaxson left and I can't even function. The house is in shambles, the kids are almost out of control, I'm exhausted and we are missing him like crazy. Reality has set in and I'm kind of realizing how much an integral role he plays in this house. I can't even change a diaper or make the babies bottle right. Maybe Jaxson wasn't as bad as I wanted him to be, and maybe, just maybe, I nagged him all too much. But still, no way on earth will my pride allow me to call him. I hate to be wrong, and you know what, I'm not wrong. I just keep it real and he can't take my realness. I'm not about to feel sorry for him and second-guess what I was doing to him. After much contemplation, I decided I wasn't calling his ass to apologize for anything or to ask him to come home. The boys and I will be just fine. I'll admit, I had some difficulty adjusting to this "single" life for the past few days but I'll learn to adjust. The struggle was real and the last two days have been very rough doing everything alone but I couldn't let my self crash.

I guess now I can see life through Jaxson's eyes. I cooked the boys' breakfast, got them dressed to drop them to the bus stop, and to take the baby to day care. Not my cup of tea but who else was going to do it? Before the boys got out of the car, I stopped and rejoiced because, even in the heat of all my anxiety, I was happy that I was able to at least get some joy from being with my babies. Jaxson is the one who spends most of the time with them and I guess I had taken even them for granted. I never realized how much I was missing watching them grow. I turned on something other than Gospel music at my son's request and we set out for their bus stop. My youngest son was doing his usual baby babbling in his car seat while the other two were beat-bopping to the jams and it seemed as if my baby was seconds away from blurting his first real words. So, I turned down the radio to see if I heard him clearly. I think he was trying to call me by my name, Mommy Nikki. I was happy he was about to say my name first before his dad's. "Na-gi-nee-kee," sounded so cute as he said it slowly, pointing at me. I heard him say it a few more times but I could not understand him clearly. Again he repeated, "Na-gi-nee-keee." Finally, I turned to my oldest son with a satisfying smile on my face. "What is your little brother trying to say to mommy because I can't make it out, but it sounds like he's saying Mommy Nikki." Then, my oldest son struggled to crack a smile, looking a bit embarrassed as he explained what my baby was saying. He stuttered, then, twitching his face, he muttered, "Mom, he's not saying Mommy Nikki, he is saying, "Nagging Nikki, Nagging Nikki."

"What?! Nagging Nikki?" I yelled angrily. I almost cursed. "Where on earth would he get that name from?"

"He gets it from Dad because that's the name Dad calls you every day. That's the name we ALL call you.

"Why would you call me that?" I asked calmly.

"Because all you do is Nag. Nagging Nikki."

I felt like shit, but I knew it was the truth. I looked at my son, turned around and nagged at him the rest of the way!

Dear Nikki,

One thing a man hates is a woman who complains about everything. Men do a lot of things to annoy women and if we had a kit guide that taught us how to build our perfect man, I think we'd all be in line trying to understand the instructions. But let's be real. There is no perfect man and there will never be. And you know what, he doesn't need to be perfect. He only needs to be perfect for you, depending on your perspective of perfection, it's all relative.

Relationships are about team work, but people also need time for themselves. Absence makes the heart grow fonder so it's OK to give your man a break every now and again; this gives him a chance to miss you and yearn for you, and perhaps to regroup and recharge.

Allow him to be a man. To be your man... and you'll see how much he appreciates the respect you have for him in the long run. Women can get a little carried away with micro-managing their man, especially if he doesn't do what we want, when we want, and how we want, but, in the end, he's a man and you can't tell him what to do. We have to talk with them, and not at them. And, bear in mind, what you give is what you get. They are not our little puppets on a string, we can't toss them around like effigies, they are people, they are men, they have feelings, too, and they are real. So, let's not treat them anyway less than that.

Sincerely,

Juliet C.

Dear Readers,

Some of the greatest moments that women share are shared with the one we love. To have a healthy, thriving and successful relationship is so important and it's often what defines our true happiness. Through creating each character, I thought of ways in which I can share the "secrets" of having a relationship that is ideal and perfect--the kind of relationship that every woman dreams of--but, truth is, there is no relationship that exists of such. Those happily-ever-afters are only found in fairy tales. So, instead, I thought I'd share the ultimate secret--and that secret is the inner jewel that lives in you. There's a jewel in every woman. A jewel: hard on the outside and rough around its edges! Very often it shines so bright that it can't always see clearly. But it's so much more than that. It's also smooth, polished, precious and rare. Nothing can compare to a true jewel. Just like a jewel, women have those same flaws and also those same great qualities --and women also has the power to make a man stay or leave and can determine if the relationship is worth fighting for or worth letting go. So now, you don't just have the power but you also have the secrets--The Secrets of a Jewel.

JuJu Jewels

We've seen from the 13 characters in this book that there are many flaws that lead to a lack of harmony in our relationships with men. The common mistakes of these ladies of drinking, cheating, nagging, being sexless and failing to commit, among others, provide us with examples of how to not give in to the same negative patterns.

Ladies, we can be sparkling jewels if we follow a few words of wisdom provided for all these character types described in this book. These *Secrets Of A Jewel* I've offered as advice will help you gain control of yourself, your man and your relationship.

Before we leave our connection here, I also offer you some JuJu Jewels of advice to maximize your understanding of the *Secrets Of A Jewel*.

♥ **Communicate with each other**

Good communications isn't something we are all born with --- something that I think some people forget. This powerful tool is something we learn during our upbringing and just life experiences overall. If you truly believe that, you will understand why having patience with others in communication is so important.

The reality check is that no other person on the planet had the exact upbringing and life experiences as you. When entering a relationship, I believe communication is one of the most important values you both should share.

Communication is the foundation of any relationship. It dictates the overall direction of the relationship, whether positive or negative. Without good communication, there can be no growth. If you find yourself in a bad space within your relationship, I challenge you to go back to the basics.

Keeping in mind your partner will NOT communicate EXACTLY like you or how you would like, take the initiative to see their perspective and find a healthy middle ground. "The best lessons in life are those learned through pure experience.

♥   **Building best friends first**

What does "best friends" mean to you? To me it is being able to finish each other's sentences, building a book full of priceless memories, having jokes only you two understand, having someone you can tell any and everything to without judgment, someone you know can even end up with the same mug shot as you!

Establishing a friendship prior to a relationship is so important. It's the beginning of "the connecting of the minds." It's more than just seeing if you're compatible physically; it's seeing if you're compatible mentally and emotionally.

You must look past that stigma of finding someone to go through the rest of your life with. Anyone can do that and not be happy. The true test is going through life's growing pains with one another and being able to GROW as a UNIT. You must have what that person lacks and vise versa, hence that's why opposites attract.

If you both were exactly the same, well what could you learn from one another? Absolutely nothing. Make your best friend your boyfriend. Not your boyfriend you best friend. Think about that.

♥   **Keep the fun in your relationship**

I hear so many women say a long-lasting relationship is hard to come by. Truth is, it isn't. Sometimes it's all about applying what you know to a new situation. We've all heard laughter is food for the soul right? It's time to apply that to your relationship.

Your relationship should be fun, the type of fun you had with your childhood friend at a slumber party at the of the day. NO ONE wants to argue all the time. Ladies, we may not understand men ALL the time, but if you don't like arguing, it's safe to say he doesn't either.

Bottom line, keep the fun brewing in your relationship and learn to pick your battles. Give yourself a double pat on the back if your mate is your best friend.

Bonus Chapter

Insecure Isabella

As a child, my mother always impressed upon me that women are very powerful human beings blessed with the innate ability to be seen and not heard. "Isabella, you can walk into the loudest room, sit quietly without uttering one word and everyone would notice you," she'd say. My grace and beauty would make all the noise, according to her. Truth is, I never really felt as if I had either of the two, no grace, no beauty.

Now, here it is, at the age of 30, the only thing my silence has done is to have left me single and friendly. I was tired of being little quiet Isabella who sits in a corner with no one ever noticing me except for my big figure. I was tired of being labeled the "quiet, fat, pretty girl."

Having a little more meat on my bones than most women always made me feel as if I had to compensate for my appearance. I had to do a little more and go that extra mile just to be seen. If I had the confidence I probably would have gone really far but, instead, I kept it simple and tried to avoid attracting unnecessary attention.

For me, going a little further would be as simple as wearing a fitted dress or putting on mascara. Well, compared to what I was accustomed to, that was a lot. I figured, however, that that's what needed to be done in order for me to find true love. All of my friends who had their men or who were in some kind of committed relationships were those "over- the-top type women." They were loud and boisterous in every way, from the way they wore their hair to the twitch in their hips. When they walked into a room they owned it and commanded attention from every eye present.

As for me, my relationships in the past would fail because obviously I was never the "It Girl." I was never sexy enough, never funny, never stylish, never much of anything enough and that was the part of me that needed to change if I was ever going to get the attention I wanted. As an adult, it was time to put away my childish life's lessons and stupid advice my mom had given me. It was time for me to grow up, make my mistakes and create these reality lessons for myself. And, boy, did I have a big lesson I was about to learn.

Here it was: The morning after my unemployment finally ended I lay in bed and was ready for something different. The mere thought of returning to corporate America after being on a hiatus for the last four months was terrifying. I dreaded working because I always felt like I was never good at any job I did. Over the past few months I had become extremely comfortable with waking up after 10 a.m., eating a few bowls of cereal in bed, catching all the latest online sales while at the same time depleting the little bit of savings I had left. I was obsessed with buying toys for my cats and clothing for my dogs. Perhaps it might've sounded better had I been shopping for myself but I was resolute to lose a few pounds first, so I'd go animal shopping instead. I was determined for the past three years but this time I was very serious. Every time I wanted to go on that diet to lose weight I would stop myself when I realized that nobody was paying me any attention anyway, so why even bother?

My priorities were all over the place. I just needed to align myself with my goals and set up a simple, workable agenda. No daytime show soap opera or dressing up my puppies could save me and occupy my time anymore. I yearned for the attention of a man and not these fur cats that huddled next to me every night. Instead, I longed to be cuddled up next to a firm frame. So, in spite of my fears, I saddled up, put on an air of confidence and headed to the job temp agency.

I was a regular at the temp agency and they were probably missing me after my long break from my last termination. Just like a man, I couldn't keep a job either. I was never noticed at work. I was good at all kinds of things but nobody ever really paid any attention to my skills or accomplishments, probably because I didn't command it. Well, today I was on a different agenda.

The agency called me last week about a few positions that were open; one included a temporary secretary for a very prominent government official. I was shocked that they had called me. Well, perhaps if they actually saw me in person to see how fat and unappealing I was, then they might change their minds. This time, though, I was anticipating something different, something more promising and nothing that I was already used to. I was poised for some risk-taking, to step outside my little comfort zone and embrace all that was awaiting me.

The night before I was all set. I had my clothes laid out and was ready to start afresh. I donned a royal-blue checkered pants suit, pulled my hair neatly in a tight bun, applied a light touch of makeup and a flat comfortable pair of black toe-less shoes. I aimed for a simple yet professional look, nothing outrageous or flattering. I'm not sexy and have never considered myself as such, but I try. "Speak less, it says more." I could still hear my mother's popular maxim resounding in my ears. I wanted to get out and be different but I felt safe this way. This was my little world, and so I decided to go with my usual flow. I drove all the way to the agency, a nervous wreck, not knowing what to expect. And my mind, as usual, was in overdrive. If he were handsome, I'm assuming I would have no worries. All that would mean is this: He wouldn't pay my fat ass any attention. I would probably end up as the coffee girl; the pick up my clothes from the cleaners' girl; the walk my dog or the order lunch girl. That was how most of my tasks ended up being at all previous jobs. I was usually given secondary, non-essential, janitorial-like or personal tasks. Some required more background work while the others forced me to function in the shadows where I didn't have to be seen or talked to. Well, I really didn't mind that at all.

I walked into the building, bubbling with confidence--my type of confidence, that is. I was greeted by a handsome male security guard at the front desk whose head was partially bowed all that time as he played on his phone. He quickly glanced at me as I wrote my name on the sign-in sheet. I soon realized that I had never seen him here before but I liked what I saw. His glance was so quick that he never even noticed me. My system was all too immune to this kind of behavior, so I immediately took a seat and waited to be called.

The minutes whisked by quickly. I watched as the security guard picked up the sign-in sheet and stared at it intently. From his facial expressions, it was obvious that he must have noticed my name because I'm sure as faith that it wasn't my face. "Isabella. Isabella White. Wow! I can't believe it's really you. Insecure Isabella." Then I observed him closer and realized that I had recognized him, too. "You look the exact same way from high school, Isabella," he said. Deep down I felt a bit uncomfortable. That was no damn compliment at all. To look the same way from high school, especially in my case, wasn't at all flattering. Well, perhaps it was the name that he remembered, the name everyone called me. "Insecure Isabella." I despised being called torturous, degrading names that the bullies made up for me in high school. I smiled politely and pretended as if it didn't bother me. I was almost rooted to the spot, hardly able to speak. I was staring right into the eyes of Chris Dawson. My high school bully;

well, one of them. I liked him despite the fact that he picked on me daily. There he was looking just as youthful and sexy as he did when we were teenagers. The only thing, he was now a grown man. But, as unattractive as I think I am, he was staring me up and down, a sign that he still had that boyish, immature trait hidden beneath those uniforms. Then, I quickly glanced at his fingers. No ring, really now! No family pictures at his desk. How could a man looking this good be single? What did it matter anyway? He wasn't thinking about me and I shouldn't be thinking about him either. After all, this was a man who made me feel like shit every day and made my high school days miserable. I knew I didn't stand a chance, but I was wallowing in a temporary euphoric fantasy. He must have caught me drifting into my thoughts. "Isabella, are you there?" he said with a light chuckle and a patronizing facial expression. "I'm sorry, Chris, how have you been?' I responded, embarrassed.

In the 10 minutes we spoke, he went on to tell me about his life and how it had turned out over the years. He was single but not interested in mingling--at least not with me. "Isabella White!" The secretary yelled. It was my turn. Chris jumped up and stretched across to give me a huge hug and to let me know how good it was seeing me. He wrapped his arms around me; well, he attempted, but his hands could barely wrap around my huge back as he tried to embrace me. At least he tried. He must have seen how embarrassed I felt because he quickly patted my shoulders reassuringly and smiled. I wasn't clueless about men or hugs, kisses or affection. At almost 30 years old, I had had boyfriends before and had even had sex with a few of them, but it wasn't anything serious. It was just random sex acts or giving in to guys I liked very much but who never cared a rat's ass about me or liked me as much as I liked them. I was that desperate girl who always brought men gifts or food, or would let them borrow money and never returned it. The girl who never really meant much to anybody. I was the big, fat, hulk-shouldered girl who was good for sleeping with just for sexual gratification and nothing more.

As Chris hugged me, it was the first in a long time that I had actually felt special. I felt as if he had missed me or was genuinely happy to see me. That tiny, insignificant gesture made me feel really great on the inside. "Man, I thought you were dead," he said, with a mischievous look on his face. "Dead, what in the world would make you think that?" I replied, very perturbed. "Did you read about me in the obituaries?" People from high school had heard all kinds of stories about me... like I was a cat lady, I had no kids, I had dropped out of college, I couldn't keep a job but, damn, dead? I never thought that they'd think I was dead. Chris went on to explain. "Someone said you were morbidly obese and died from a heart attack. But, I'm glad that that was only a rumor." I was crushed. Whatever little confidence I was working with was definitely gone. The only thing that was what was dead, was my damn confidence!

I made my way to the back office and the entire time all I thought about was Chris' words. I couldn't believe he thought I was dead all this time. I knew I was huge and probably looking like a zombie but, dead? Then it dawned on me. Maybe Chris was being his usual self, cracking jokes and trying to hurt my feelings. I really hoped so because as unsightly as I was I wasn't dead and neither did I look like someone who was dying.

The clerk at the agency informed me that the job was mine and that I would start my training for the position first thing in the morning. As I exited the office, Chris was still playing on his phone. I hurried out quickly so as not to see him because I didn't want him to see my grim figure hobbling out the exit. It seemed that I was trying too hard because as I sneaked out the door, my wide hips knocked a woman's hot coffee out of her hand as she made her way through the same entrance. I was mortified. Chris heard the commotion and jumped up with his usual dramatic and overbearing self, grabbing the fire extinguisher and creating a terrifying scene. He sprang over the desk and pointed the nuzzle at me. "It's just coffee, calm down, Chris!" I said, trying to add a little finesse to my voice. I was in no mood to be sprayed nor to be made a fool of by Chris, in the same manner he did for years in high school. The entire office was staring at me. I felt even more horrible when I recalled the moment he had asked me to the prom and never came to pick me up after I spent three hours getting dressed. He was definitely trying to embarrass me again and I wasn't buying into it. After so many years this loser was still at it. So, I walked out of the office quickly and ignored the dumb smirk on his face.

I hurried to my car and headed home with my plan in motion. On my way home I stopped by the mall to pick up a new outfit for my new position tomorrow. He had made me so angry that I was ready to doll up myself and see the expression on his dumb face. I even decided to treat myself to a manicure and pedicure because tomorrow would be a new day, and I was ready to put on my big girl panties and show Chris who I really was.

The next morning, I woke up extra early to let my hair down from that tight, neat bun. I slowly and carefully made some tight curls with each piece of hair. Then, I gently applied some delicate, light colored make-up and powered my face. The mascara was neat, eye-liner was on point, eye brows were neatly sculpted and I topped it all off with a sexy pink lipstick and a splash of blush. I wasn't a big makeup person but I spent enough time practicing at home or playing make up in my mirror to know exactly how to fix myself beautifully.

Of course, I was not leaving out my tight fitting girdle. All that was left were my sexy hips, looking curvy and shapely. I pulled up the new black dress I had bought and loved the fit. It hugged me perfectly. It was professional and sexy, knee length and stretched across, hugging every inch of my body. A little cleavage was popping up and so I made sure to add a little sparkle lotion across my chest as my breasts sat nicely in my new dress. Then, I pulled up my fishnet tights on my large sexy legs and placed my well-manicured feet in my sexy suede pumps. I was scared of falling in these heels, but this look was worth the fear and tumble. Finally, my mom's words echoed. "Beauty really was silent, and my look was making all the noise." I never felt more confident in my life. Something finally evolved inside of me and I felt amazing.

I dabbed on my new perfume and headed to the car. During the entire ride I blasted my music and drove excitedly to the office. It took me a little while to get from the car to the door, as I was not quite used to walking in heels. But I managed to make it in time, and just fine. I felt a tad nervous as I drew closer to the entrance. I stood there for a minute, checking my makeup through the translucent glass door. I looked amazing and that girdle was working miracles for me, miraculously taking away 15 pounds. I took a long, deep breath and then walked inside. Chris was playing on his phone again. My perfume was so loud that the wind transported the aroma from my body and straight onto Chris' nose. He looked up, "Damn, damn...Wow! You clean up well."

I ignored him and asked him to buzz me in the back so I could get to the office to meet my new boss. He arose from his desk and walked around to the entrance, this time with no fanfare or drama, characteristic of him. I didn't need for him to get up, so I wasn't quite sure of his intention, but I remained non-judgmental and calm. I was saving my voice this time for when I needed it. "Baby, let's start over. Let's leave high school where high school was," he said, staring me up and down. I was speechless. I wondered why Chris was calling me baby and suddenly being super sweet. I felt flattered but I knew that his intentions were malicious. So, I remained calm.

I answered politely, "Sure, you're right, we can start over." Chris smiled broadly while extending his arm. "I like that. Hi, gorgeous, my name is Chris, what's yours?" I held my hand out to Chris', not sure of what to make of this unusual and questionable gesticulation. I thought for a minute and then I decided how I'd respond. "Hi, I'm Insecure Isabella," I said provocatively. "Remember her?"

Chris just stood there, looking stupid and confused in his soiled security uniform. I held my head high, swung my manicured fingers in the air, pursed my lips and walked away looking fierce and fabulous with my curves and all!

Dear Isabella,

When a woman is unsure of herself almost anyone can tell. Her actions read, INSECURE. Often times, we spend so much time admiring the exterior beauty of others without truly admiring the external depth, their truest beauty.

Society is responsible for what we view as beauty. You have to be thin, but not too skinny; a little weight on your hips but they shouldn't be too wide; you can't have a waist; your legs must be straight; your walk must be attractive; your hair must be laid; and all 32 of your teeth have got to be perfectly straight and white. But what do you view as beautiful?

"Look in the mirror and love yourself," is a comment I've always disliked. It seems so easy for someone to tell you to look in the mirror and love what you see. I think people don't realize that you can't love what you don't like looking at, though.

Here's what I suggest when you look in the mirror and you don't love what you see on the outside: Change it! Fix whatever it is you hate until you love what you see. But I can almost guarantee that if what's broken is really internal, then either way it won't help. Truth is, when you really look in the mirror we may not like who we are on the outside, but what we hate most is the person we see on the inside. We hate to see the person staring us in our face and screaming our truth. We see the pain we've endured and the pain we've caused others to endure, the person we are not but would love to be, the lies we've told and the ugly truth we've heard. We hate seeing that one person who knows who you really are. We hate seeing them so much that we don't even look them in the eyes. You become your biggest critic and you stare, searching for something beautiful. And you never find it.

So love what you see, and change what you hate seeing. Whether it's in or out! This isn't to say don't change who you are and don't embrace your flaws, but there's also nothing wrong with enhancement.

Being natural is gorgeous because it's who you are. However, if you feel good about jazzing your beauty up a tad, letting your hair down, wearing some extensions or even putting on some fake eye lashes, go for it but make sure you know where your truest beauty lies.

What good would it be to plant a fake flower in artificial soil? So that it could just look pretty? It would be like having beauty you can only see but not feel. Remember, true beauty really does lie in the eyes of the beholder, and those eyes are looking at what's on the inside, too.

So, if you want to stop hating how you look, and do away with all your insecurities, make your heart beautiful. That's the greatest beauty to desire.

Sincerely,

Juliet C.

ABOUT THE AUTHOR

Juliet C., affectionately known as Juju, was born in Brooklyn, N.Y. As a child, Juliet developed a passion for the arts and a love for creative writing. She spent her summers perfecting her craft by writing poetry, short stories and plays. After meeting her fiancé, she became particularly interested in the quality of relationships and true love. Taking social media by storm, she began sharing advice on several topics for her large fan base. Best known for her advice, "Juju Jewels" sought to strengthen confidence in women, while also exploring the commonalities of flawed relationships.

After receiving positive reviews from her advice columns, Juliet realized that many women found her advice column beneficial. And so, by popular demand, she turned her advice into a concept and began writing her first of many series entitled *Secrets Of A Jewel*.